BLIND BEAUTY

And Other Tales of Redemption

BY

MEREDITH LEIGH BURTON

BLIND BEAUTY AND OTHER TALES OF REDEMPTION

Cover Design by Hannah Williams
Interior Design by Savannah Jezowski of Dragonpenpress.com

ISBN: 978-1720301288

Printed and Published in the United States of America
10 9 8 7 6 5 4 3 2 1

Table of Contents

Dedication

To those who walk in darkness but seek light.

When Jesus spoke again to the people, He said, "I am the light of the world. He who follows Me will never walk in darkness but have the light of life."

John 8:12

DEDICATION

With inexpressible thanks to Jesus Christ, the One who planted
the rose of love in my heart.

And to Dr. Mila Truan, the teacher who opened the eyes in my
fingertips as she taught me to read Braille.
Her dedication carried me through a gateway into journeys I'll
always treasure.

PART 1: TWO ROSES

CHAPTER ONE

J enna strolled through the lush meadows, delighting in the soft song of the grass beneath her feet. She listened for any sound that would herald someone following her, but she heard no one to hinder her walk. She sighed in relief. Songbirds serenaded her in joyous trills, and the scent of spring was redolent upon the air. Spring was her favorite season, the time when the land of Floraine radiated new life. It was the season when flowers and trees awoke from sleep and praised Tecoptra for his goodness. She remembered a proverb Mother had always been fond of murmuring: "The fragrance of spring is the fragrance of love." Spring had been Mother's favorite season too.

As Jenna ascended the small hillock before her, she felt a thrill of anticipation. Her destination lay just ahead. She remembered how she used to admire the profusion of pink and white blossoms upon the majestic apple trees. Now she had to rely upon her ears, which brought to her the rustling music of the trees' songs. Anger at the injustice threatened to rise and mar the beautiful morning, so she forced it back.

Jenna entered the apple orchard, brushing the sturdy stick she carried along the ground. Poppa had carved the guidance tool for her. As she walked, the tool encountered obstacles that would have caused her to fall. Thus she was able to avoid accidents.

As Jenna shuffled onward, a soft sound stole upon her: the sound of weeping. The piteous cries issued from her appointed destination.

Jenna was drawn to the cries. Hadn't she made those moans of desolation only six months earlier? Shaking, she followed the sounds to her tree.

When trouble began stalking her family, Jenna had sought refuge in the orchard that lay beyond the village. Her tree was a perfect sanctuary. Jenna named it the Tree with the Humped Back, for it bent at an awkward angle. Even so, there was no denying its majesty.

The Tree with the Humped Back was sacred in Jenna's mind. Before the fire occurred, she had often come here to read.

Jenna approached the tree, compassion filling her heart. Softly, she asked, "Why're you crying?"

"Go away!" A boy's snarling voice reached her ears.

Jenna involuntarily shuddered, for the voice was harsher than any she'd ever heard. Then she admonished herself for being silly.

"Are you all right?" she asked.

She heard thudding footfalls as someone stepped from behind the tree. "Go away," the boy repeated. "Why aren't you running?"

Fear was receding in favor of indignation. After all, she was trying to help. "Why should I leave? This is my tree."

"I was here first," the boy said indignantly.

Jenna heard the sadness beneath the harsh tones of the boy's voice. Despite her frustration, she decided to be polite. She groped within the pocket of her threadbare frock. She withdrew two pieces of peppermint candy and popped one into her mouth. She also retrieved a small handkerchief. Holding forth her offerings, Jenna said around the melting sweetness, "These peppermint drops always comfort me. My sister makes them. She sells them at market. Would you like one?"

There was a long pause. Then Jenna felt a brief touch against her palm. She shivered at the touch, for the hand was strangely heavy. When its hold was relinquished, the peppermint had been taken. She still held the handkerchief.

The boy spoke again, his voice emerging from behind the tree. "That's a girl's handkerchief."

Jenna laughed. "So?"

"I don't need your help. Why're you pestering me?"

Enough was enough! "If you've nothing civil to say, then leave! You're ruining my alone time." Jenna trailed her hands along her tree's crooked trunk. She placed her feet upon the lowest branch and began to climb. Her hands and legs shook with weakness as she pulled herself upward. Yet she was determined.

Ah! Here was her branch at last. She sat and began swinging her legs as she caught her breath. "I know you're still there," she called cheekily.

"If you don't go away, I'll make the tree let you go."

Jenna felt a shiver stroke her spine. "What do you mean?"

"I'll break the branch. You'll fall."

Jenna snorted, an unladylike but appropriate sound given the circumstances. "You're a ninny. You have no power over trees. They wouldn't listen to a stuck-up—"

She felt the tree move, a sharp thrusting motion as if it were pushing against her. Jenna gasped. The tree moved yet again, and a snapping sound filled her ears. She plummeted toward the ground.

She felt two strange hands grip her sides, halting her fall. She was gently lowered to the ground. The hands felt like large paws, but her mind spun in confusion, and she wondered if she was imagining this fact. She stumbled as she tried to regain her bearings and brushed against something sharp with many prongs. She flinched.

Jenna heard the grass rustle as the boy moved next to her. "You shouldn't have said that." His voice trembled. "You can't see, can you?"

Jenna didn't speak. She was too frightened. Frantically, she groped for her guidance tool, which had dropped to the ground. She gasped when her exploring fingers touched a severed branch that lay beneath the tree. "How could you?" she whispered.

She felt her stick being placed within her hand. "I was only trying to frighten you. I'll leave now," the boy said.

Jenna stepped away from the tree. Swallowing, she said, "I'm sorry I called you a ninny. You weren't letting me help. Poppa and Mirabel are like that, and it makes me mad. Are you a Flower Master? I thought only grown-ups spoke to flora."

"Claudio says Flower Masters can be any age. Trees and flowers are my friends. I talk to this one every time I come here, and he talks to me. Now he'll probably never speak to me again. He's furious."

As if to confirm his words, the tree's branches rustled violently, several apple blossoms falling to the ground as it did so.

"I've made him cry," the boy whispered sadly.

"This tree's my friend," Jenna said. "I never thought it would try to hurt me."

6

"He wouldn't have on his own. He says he's sorry. So am I." After another long silence, the boy said, "I'm glad you cannot see."

Jenna blinked, unsure what to say. She thought of the fire. "It's hard," she said. Then, to distract herself, she asked, "Will you tell me why you were crying when I found you?"

"I wasn't crying," he growled.

Jenna sighed. "I'm not dimwitted."

"Maybe I was crying, but you would too if your father told you not to leave the house and threatened to lock you in."

Empathy stirred within Jenna's heart. "But, you did leave," she pointed out.

"I snuck out. The roses helped me. The servants'll be searching."

Jenna leant forward, whispering conspiratorially, "I snuck out too."

It was then that Jenna heard footfalls and a frantic cry. She felt her arm being jerked.

"Catch him!" Poppa's hoarse voice yelled.

Jenna struggled against Poppa's grip, crying out in indignation.

She heard shouts as a large crowd approached her. She heard someone running and the twang of bowstrings and the whoosh of arrows. A low whimper stole upon her ears. Poppa lifted her into his arms. He began running, paying no heed to his daughter's angry flailings.

When Jenna was finally placed upon the ground, she snarled, "How did you find me? I thought you'd gone to help mend Ms. Carruthers' roof."

Poppa spoke through clenched teeth. "Confound you, girl! Thank Tecoptra's providence, I forgot my tools. I found Mirabel in a dreadful state. She said she went next door to give Charlotte some mint syrup for the baby's cough. She'd only just returned and couldn't find you. Can't we leave you even for a minute? What were you thinking?"

"I'm sick of being cooped up, Poppa. You won't let me go anywhere."

"That's not true. You accompany Mirabel to market every time she goes."

"Yes, and what do I do there?" Jenna's voice shook. "I sit on a stool and swing my legs. People cluck at me. They're like ill-bred hens! I had to get away." She blinked rapidly, her eyes burning. Sadness burrowed into her soul like an animal unreleased. "How could you hurt that boy? I was only trying to help."

"What boy?" Poppa's voice was softer now, tinged with concern. "That beast would've killed you."

Jenna blinked. "Beast?"

Poppa clutched her hand. She felt him trembling. "A monster," he whispered. "A wolf with a deer's head."

Jenna shuddered. Poppa was many things—a worrier, a careless businessman, and a protector—but he wasn't a liar. Yet what he was saying was absurd, wasn't it? She thought of the boy's touch. Had she been imagining it, or had his hand felt paw-like? Shaking, she allowed Poppa to lead her home.

CHAPTER TWO

Paul ran, his paws padding upon the soft earth. His sides heaved with exertion. He knew the arrow had simply grazed his shoulder. Yet fear coursed through him in relentless waves. What if they found him? Was the girl all right?

"Oh, Tecoptra spare me!"

Paul sagged in relief as the familiar voice broke upon his ears. He saw Claudio's weathered face and worried frown. The elderly servant hobbled toward his master's son with many rheumatic cursings. Paul stopped running to allow the servant to reach him.

"You'll be the death of me, boy!"

Paul growled threateningly, but the angry sound only made Claudio laugh. "Don't call me *boy*," Paul snarled.

"Don't know what else to call someone who disobeys his father's orders." Claudio held out a heavily veined hand, gently touching Paul's shoulder. "He's only trying to protect you."

"I don't want protection. I just want—" Paul stopped speaking. He didn't know what he wanted. After a moment, he told Claudio of his encounter with the girl and the incident with the tree. "The tree said he obeyed me because my anger flowed into him. He couldn't control what he did. I didn't mean to hurt her. Her face was so sad, and she had scars around her eyes. She was so nice, and she didn't run away."

Claudio nodded, his brown eyes filled with concern. "It's fortunate she wasn't hurt. The tree recognized you as master. Now I think I understand how you've been escaping. I'll make a bargain with you."

Paul stiffened. "Bargain?"

"Yes. Your father insists you stay in your room, and, for a Flower Master, that's akin to death. I'll ask him to allow you to walk within the garden every day."

Paul scowled. "You've tried that before."

Claudio smiled. "But now you've given me proof of what you are. I think he'll listen this time." He lifted his hand, turning so that his gaze fell upon the vast array of apple trees. "I must take you home. Close your eyes."

"I won't be put to sleep this time. You can't make me," Paul snarled.

"I haven't a choice. You know your father." Claudio softly addressed the trees. "Summon a zephyr to conduct us home."

Instantly, the trees began rustling their branches in obedience to the order, and a gentle breeze began to blow. The zephyr wrapped itself around Paul's body, cradling him like an infant. He struggled against the breeze, but it held him firm. Finally, Paul's eyes closed, and he sank into a deep slumber.

The zephyr lifted him from the ground. It bore him away, and Claudio followed in the zephyr's wake until Paul was deposited before a shimmering gate.

Claudio surveyed the gate before him.

It was an enchanted gate that he had erected himself. Only he or the sentries posted within the grounds could open it. Claudio murmured some words, and the gate opened soundlessly. The zephyr lifted Paul once again, ushering him inside and laying him upon the ground.

A cobblestoned walkway bordered by rosebushes of red and white gleamed before Claudio's eyes. As Claudio stepped onto the path, the gate closed behind him.

"You've found him, have you?" A stout man emerged from a clump of rosebushes. The man's emerald eyes sparked with anger. "What trouble has he caused? Did he attack someone?"

"He's hurt, master." Claudio pointed to Paul's sleeping form.

The man flinched and bent to examine Paul's shoulder. "How long will he sleep? Did you make him forget his time outside?"

Claudio sighed. "He'll sleep for an hour. When he awakens, he won't remember leaving here. It's against my better judgment to continue casting memory charms, master. One day, they'll no longer work, and we'll suffer for it; you mark my words."

The man frowned. "You wouldn't have to resort to charms if you'd just listen to me. The wound's not serious. Bandage it and take him to his room. Be certain to lock his door."

"I won't subject him to imprisonment."

The man glared. "You'll obey me or seek another situation."

Claudio smiled at this bluff. He was threatened with firing at least twice a day. "How will you keep an eye on him without me, Gustav?"

Gustav glared, but his voice was resigned when he said, "Just make sure he doesn't escape again. He could've been killed."

11

"Don't you think I know that? He did what any self-respecting boy would do. Wouldn't you want freedom? Why won't you let him be a child?"

"Because he's not a child. That witch saw to that." Gustav spoke harshly even as tears shimmered in his eyes.

Claudio flinched. "Gwendolyn isn't a witch. She's a Flower Mistress. She didn't realize the implications of her actions. Magic is unpredictable, and she was young. I believe Paul is a Flower Master too. That's how he's been escaping. He talks to the roses of his longing to leave here, and they grant his request."

Gustav stared. "Then instruct them to stop. Don't you have more control over them than he does?"

Claudio nodded, but he fidgeted nervously. "The ability to converse with flora is a gift from Tecoptra. To interfere with it is wrong. He has a purpose in giving Paul that gift."

"Don't speak to me of this so-called Tecoptra. I've no patience with myths. If he exists, he certainly doesn't care about our plight."

"I think he cares more than you know. Why else would he take the trouble to give Paul such a gift? Your son is lonely, Gustav. The flowers are his only companions. Tecoptra doesn't want Paul to be confined like an animal in a cage. He wants him to grow up like any normal person."

Gustav's face crumpled, and he stared at his sleeping son, his shoulders shaking. "Paul may behave like a child, but it doesn't change how he looks. People only care about what they can see. That's life, and the sooner we accept that truth, the better. I'm Paul's father, and I'll determine what's best for him. Take him to his room, and this time, make sure he stays there."

"I shall, if you'll make me a promise." Claudio's tone was stern. Gustav had no choice but to listen. His servant, who had served his father and grandfather before him, was wise and knew much.

"What promise?"

"You'll allow Paul to walk in this garden. I'll ensure that no one sees him, but he must have some freedom. He's already becoming more agitated than is wise."

Gustav shook his head. "He's escaped once too often. These so-called sentries of yours are supposed to put him to sleep if he tries to escape." He glared accusingly at the rosebushes. They drooped their heads in embarrassment.

Claudio glared in frustration. He began to pace. He'd served this family for years, being careful to conceal his magical abilities. When the change had come upon Paul, Claudio had no choice but to offer his help. He loved Gustav like a son, but Gustav treated magic like it was his own personal possession. He never considered the dangers.

Finally, Claudio said, "You expect too much of me, Gustav. I'm a paltry enchanter at best, and I've done all I can. I won't interfere with Tecoptra's will. To do so is madness."

Gustav stared at Claudio for a long moment. "If you won't help me, I'll find someone who will. Take him inside." He turned and stamped away.

Claudio could not contain his tears. He trudged toward a majestic castle that towered beyond the rosebushes, a castle that should have been a home but was instead a prison. "Forgive me," he murmured to Paul, whom the zephyr was now bearing toward the castle.

He addressed the roses. "If he asks to leave here again, don't let him go." The roses rustled a promise to obey, but the sound contained a heavy reproach. Claudio sighed.

Then, thanking the zephyr, he gathered Paul into his arms as he was deposited on the threshold. Claudio entered the castle, the door slamming behind him with a reverberating finality.

CHAPTER THREE

A middle-aged woman stood by the closed castle gate. She listened for any sound from within, but all was still. Pain patrolled the grounds like a sentry.

Gwendolyn shook with sobs, and she repeatedly traced a hand along her left cheek. She thought of the crimson birthmark that gleamed there. In her other hand, she held a white rose. As she stood by the gate, she remembered the evil she had inadvertently caused. If Gwendolyn was honest with herself, perhaps she had known all along that her hatred would wreak havoc. Now, she hoped in some small way to make amends. The white rose she held would hopefully set things right.

Gwendolyn had always possessed an affinity for flowers. They were kind. They never laughed at her. She understood their language. Flowers imparted their wisdom and brought her comfort. In return, she lavished love upon them, discovering even as a child that she was able to use them to bring joy to others.

Gwendolyn hadn't meant to hurt anyone. She especially hadn't meant to hurt Gustav. As the pain-cloaked silence enveloped her, she sank into her memories.

The fact that Gustav was a duke's son mattered not at all to Gwendolyn. She'd met him at the market one day, he a stout young man of seventeen then, she a maiden of sixteen. Mother allowed Gwendolyn to sell flowers at market, for her work as an herbalist brought in little. Since Father's death, Gwendolyn helped in any way she could.

Of course, few people bought her wares. Everyone knew of the birthmark. Villagers passed by her stall, their eyes averted. She heard their fearful whispers. "Ain't natural, 'er so ugly and them flowers so pretty. They might be enchanted. Witch's spawn." As if Mother possessed an iota of magic!

Gustav was one of the few patrons who would purchase her wares. She knew the flowers he bought were for a sweetheart, but she didn't care. He talked with her, and she talked with him. The brief conversations brought her comfort. When his father had died, she'd empathized with his plight, and they often talked together about their families. He also shared his misgivings about becoming a duke. She remembered encouraging him, saying that he would be a wonderful ruler. Gwendolyn often cursed herself for growing attached to Gustav. She knew she was foolish, but feelings of longing haunted her, and she couldn't banish him from her mind.

She remembered how her heart had broken the day she heard of Gustav's engagement. He was to marry a nobleman's daughter named Sauda. The engagement celebration was held in the duke's castle, a building that Gwendolyn would never dare enter. But on that fateful night, she couldn't stay away.

She stole into the castle ballroom. The ball was a masquerade party, and she wore a veil that cast the mark in shadow. She had no intention of approaching Gustav. She merely wanted to see him.

In the midst of the ball, the bride-to-be spotted her. Gwendolyn remembered the haughty stare that pierced through her veil to the ghastly visage beneath. Sauda wore no mask. Her face shone with radiance. She summoned a servant. "Remove this creature from the festivities." She

16

spoke softly, but her voice carried clearly to the guests. The servant led Gwendolyn from the room amid murmurs and stares.

Gwendolyn stood outside the ballroom, her cheeks flushed. She heard footsteps behind her and turned to stare at the kind visage of a tall man. He carried a platter, which held a cake decorated with roses. Gwendolyn backed away in embarrassment. "I didn't mean to—"

"Mean to what?" The man smiled at her. "What's the harm in standing outside a door?" He turned his head down the corridor. "Help me carry things to the dessert table, will you?"

Gwendolyn blinked. "What?"

"Something wrong with your hearing?" He blinked back at her, grinning. "It's me with the hearing loss, not you." He gestured for her to follow him.

Bewildered, Gwendolyn trailed in the man's wake. They turned down numerous corridors and entered a small chamber. The man turned to face her. "He'll be here any moment," he whispered. Then he was gone.

Gwendolyn gaped, hope filling her heart. As if on cue, Gustav entered the room. His face was sad when he looked at her. "What did you mean by coming here? My fiancée is, shall we say, a bit—"

"Repulsive?" The word shot from Gwendolyn's mouth, and she immediately flushed with embarrassment. "Sorry."

Gustav frowned. "I was thinking headstrong. Look, I'm sorry too. I can't disobey Father's orders. The marriage was arranged before he died. The man who led you here is named Claudio. I've talked with him, and he says he'd be glad to help you." He held out his hand, clasping Gwendolyn's own. He smiled at her. "If you want to work here, you may. You've always been kind to me, and I want to return the favor. You don't have to work here, of course, but—" His voice trailed away, and he relinquished Gwendolyn's hand.

Gwendolyn smiled at him. "Thank you," she said. She didn't consider refusing Gustav's invitation. After all, her family needed money. Besides, she wouldn't bother Gustav. She'd just do her work, and if in the process she saw him occasionally, well, that was all right, wasn't it?

She worked in the scullery, keeping out of sight as much as possible. Everyone knew she was different, and her reclusive behavior ensured her privacy.

CHAPTER FOUR

Gwendolyn discovered that Claudio possessed the same affinity for flowers that she did. She discovered this fact on the third day of her employment.

Cook, a cantankerous man with a distaste for morning, noon, and evening, ordered Gwendolyn to take breakfast to the nobleman's daughter's room.

"Mistress Sauda wants her breakfast waitin' after her bath. Betsy has the confounded toothache again! You ask me, it's all pretense." He growled and resumed his work.

Gwendolyn turned to the large breakfast tray sitting on the counter. A bouquet of flowers sat in its center. She couldn't help smiling. Mistress Sauda had at least one good quality. She loved bouquets of all kinds. As Gwendolyn surveyed the flowers, she noticed two roses with drooping heads. "You're tired," she murmured sympathetically, bending toward the weary flowers to comfort them.

"You talk to them, do you?"

Gwendolyn started and glanced up. Her eyes met Claudio's, and he smiled at her. "They crave attention as much as people and animals do," he murmured. He turned his gaze to the roses and stroked their petals. "Buck up there, ladies. Can't have you frowning when you're presented to the prospective bride, can we?"

Gwendolyn gasped as she watched the roses move. They actually shifted beneath the elderly servant's hand as if they were waking up. She gaped at Claudio. He winked at her and approached Cook.

Gwendolyn's heart pounded with apprehension as she took the tray. She left the kitchen and traversed several maze-like corridors until she reached Sauda's room. Since her tentative knock yielded no response, she opened the door and entered the chamber, inhaling the rich aroma of apple-scented soap. Mistress Sauda was probably bathing in the adjoining chamber.

Gwendolyn placed the breakfast tray on a table beside the bed and prepared to leave. As she turned, her eyes were arrested by a gleaming vanity, upon which stood countless pots and jars. Almost involuntarily, she stepped toward the table, her gaze coming to rest upon a small hand mirror.

The mirror was carved from applewood. Semiprecious stones framed its heart-shaped face. Gwendolyn's hand closed over it before she could stop herself. Mirrors were a rarity, and she couldn't resist this one even though she knew what she'd see. She gazed into its depths, her twisted features mocking her as they were reflected back.

Quickly, Gwendolyn replaced the mirror upon the table and groped among the cosmetics until her hand closed over a vial of concealer cream. She picked it up. It was very light. No one would notice if—

"What're you doing?" The melodic voice caused Gwendolyn to start violently. The concealer fell from her shaking hands to the floor. The vial shattered into fragments. "F-forgive me, my lady. I—"

"Clean it up." Sauda turned emerald eyes onto Gwendolyn's flushed face. Her flawless skin gleamed. Her damp, chestnut hair sparkled with golden hues. "Did you hear me? Clean it up."

Gwendolyn hastened to obey. As she worked, Sauda watched her every movement with impassive intensity.

When Gwendolyn had completed her task, the girl said, "I have one more task for you to perform." She gestured to her vanity table, smiling slightly. "Do you see that yellow casket of cream? Anoint my face with a small amount."

Her cheeks flaming with humiliation, Gwendolyn began applying the thick, peppermint-scented mixture to Sauda's face. Sauda's features shimmered more than ever. Her skin glowed with vibrancy, looking exactly the way it had the night of the ball. So, Sauda *had* worn a mask, just not a traditional one. Gwendolyn gasped in shock.

Sauda smiled at her. "Now apply some to your face."

Gwendolyn's heart began to pound. Anticipation tore through her even as she hesitated, not daring to hope.

"What're you waiting for?"

Gwendolyn applied some of the cream to her face, paying particular attention to the mark upon her cheek.

Sauda watched her. "My brother made me this face cream. We can't afford luxuries like cosmetics because of Father's debts, but that doesn't matter. My brother always helps me. He's quite talented. This is a cream that enhances your features. It makes anyone who wears it beautiful." She laughed. "Well, almost anyone."

Sauda thrust her mirror into Gwendolyn's hand. Gwendolyn gasped at her face. The mark shone more lividly than ever. In fact, it seemed to have spread. Gwendolyn moaned, a broken, pitiful cry. Her head spun, and tears sprang to her eyes. She tried to blink them back, but she could not.

Sauda blinked, proffering a damp cloth. Something akin to regret crossed her features. Then they hardened.

"It's ridiculous to cry. Has it ever helped me?" She continued watching Gwendolyn, who was shaking.

Sighing, Sauda rubbed the cloth upon Gwendolyn's cheeks. "Honestly, the way you're acting, you'd think I committed murder." She finished removing the cream, and when she spoke again, her voice was flat. "You come near my fiancé, and I'll force you to wear the cream in public. Do you understand?"

Gwendolyn trembled. "I meant no harm, my lady."

"You lying witch! Gustav told me he's the one who got you the situation here. My brother told me not to worry, that Gustav wouldn't break our engagement. But how can he be sure? I have enough problems without a repulsive creature like you interfering. If Gustav doesn't marry me, I'll be sent home. I won't go back there. Father will kill me if I—I have to escape from—" Her impassive mask fell away, revealing a contorted visage of pain and fear.

Gwendolyn's mind whirled with anger. "If you knew anything about Gustav, you'd know that he's kind and honorable. Your brother was right when he told you not to worry. Gustav will marry you. I've known Gustav for months, and you know nothing about him."

Gwendolyn flung the mirror onto Sauda's dressing table. Satisfaction stabbed through her as the mirror shattered. "Perhaps Gustav will teach you some civility. I'm not pretty like you, but that doesn't mean I don't have feelings. You're a spoiled, arrogant beast who should be taught a lesson!" She bestowed one look on Sauda's stricken face and stormed from the room.

CHAPTER FIVE

The days before the wedding passed in a whirlwind. Gwendolyn worked tirelessly, ever conscious of the fact that she might be sent away at any moment. Yet nothing happened. Anger festered within her, a roiling, unquenchable fire. The only time she found relief was when she arranged flowers.

On the wedding day, the kitchen was more crowded than usual. Servants scurried about, preparing the wedding breakfast. Gwendolyn volunteered to arrange the breakfast bouquet.

Claudio turned to her, his gaze penetrating. "Thank you, Gwendolyn, but it's a special day, and I think it best if I arrange the flowers."

Gwendolyn blinked in surprise. "But don't I do adequate work?"

"Phenomenal work." He smiled at her, but beneath his smile lurked concern. "I must speak with you. We'll talk in the garden."

Gwendolyn nodded and followed Claudio outside. It was a lovely morning. Roses sparkled with dew, and the temperature was perfect. Claudio sat upon a bench and gestured for Gwendolyn to join him.

He looked at her with piercing eyes, and his voice was urgent when he said, "I need to know if you talked of your hatred of Sauda to the flowers."

Gwendolyn blinked. "No," she said.

He frowned. "You cannot lie to me. You've poisoned them."

Gwendolyn glared. "I've done nothing but love them," she said defensively.

"Exactly. Yet hatred lurks in your heart. Don't you know what you are? You're a Flower Mistress, one Tecoptra has chosen to care for his creation. You give of yourself, and the flowers accept what you give. They serve you, fulfilling your desires. When you spoke to them of your hatred for Sauda, they determined to help you. They allowed your hatred to enter their hearts."

"What do you know of anything, old man?" The words spewed forth, and guilt immediately followed. Yet Gwendolyn couldn't stop speaking. "Tecoptra is a myth. If he existed, would I look like this? Anyhow, Sauda's not the right person for Gustav."

"And who are you to decide that, young woman?" Claudio smiled compassionately upon her. "Only Tecoptra knows what's best in these situations. You must ask him to remove this hatred from you. If you don't, it will eat you alive, just as it is even now consuming the flowers' hearts. Tecoptra exists whether you believe in him or not. He gives all creation free will. Humanity, flora, and fauna can choose to serve him, or they can choose to reject him. Whatever path is chosen creates a magic that resembles the casting of a stone into water. The ripples fan outward, and one never knows what will happen as a result."

Gwendolyn turned her gaze to the roses in the garden. Something was indeed wrong with them. They huddled into themselves, convulsing with pain.

Shaking, she whispered to Claudio, "I told them Sauda needed to be taught a lesson and that her descendants would be no better than beasts. I said I wished Gustav would marry me instead of her." Blinking back tears, she turned abruptly and reentered the scullery.

During the wedding breakfast, everyone admired Sauda's beautiful gown and radiant smile. Yet certain people questioned why one of her fingers was bandaged. The servants whispered among themselves, and Gwendolyn listened to their gossip, each word slamming against her like a slap.

"Saw a red rose in her room when I brought mornin' tea," a maid whispered. "Red! Ill omen, that is. She was cryin', and I said I'd take it away, but she'd already grabbed it. Pricked her finger on a thorn, she did. I took it from her, and it wilted in my hand. Died right then. Gave me the creeps!"

Gwendolyn shuddered, the full implications of her actions finally dawning upon her. If Claudio spoke truthfully, then she'd delivered death to Sauda that morning. She'd only meant to deliver an insult. Everyone knew that white roses were the only ones brides received on wedding days. To receive any other colored flower, particularly red, was akin to the vilest insult.

Sauda grew ill the day after the wedding.

Gwendolyn sought out Claudio and confessed her wrongdoing. "How can I help her?" she asked, her voice shaking.

Claudio gazed at Gwendolyn with compassion. "You can ask Tecoptra to heal her."

"Isn't there something more I can do?"

Claudio frowned. "The poison's in her bloodstream. Physicians come daily with new remedies, but unless a miracle occurs—" His voice trailed away.

Gwendolyn bowed her head and turned to leave.

"Will you simply run from your problems, Gwendolyn?" Claudio spoke harshly, more harshly than she'd ever heard him speak. "There's no shame in praying, you know. Sometimes, it's the only thing we can do."

After a long moment, Gwendolyn nodded. She continued to work in the scullery, drawing as little attention to herself as possible. Occasionally, she'd ask Cook to prepare apple custard tart, a dessert Sauda loved. Gwendolyn arranged the dessert trays herself, placing upon them sachets of fragrant herbs that brought healing to those who possessed them.

One day, it was announced that the duke and duchess were expecting a child. Over the next several months, Sauda's illness lifted.

Then disaster struck yet again.

CHAPTER SIX

The baby was handsome. He sported a headful of russet curls, and his eyes sparkled with emerald hues. Gwendolyn heard the servants talking.

"Such an adorable little 'un, and so good-natured! Wet nurse says he hardly ever cries. Pity about the mistress. She was weak, but she looked peaceful-like when she saw him. Heard her whisper, 'Gustav saved me, and now I've given him a son.' Then she closed her eyes."

Gwendolyn wept. She knew she needed to leave the castle, to go far away before she caused more harm. Yet she couldn't leave. She would serve Gustav and his son as best she could. In that small way, perhaps she could alleviate her guilt.

Gustav named his son Paul. On Paul's second birthday, the change came upon him.

Gwendolyn shuddered as she thought of that day, a day of terror and pain. She remembered kneeling in the flower garden, removing recalcitrant weeds that were encroaching upon her charges. She'd resolved to stay as far away from flowers as possible, but that resolution had not lasted. They cried out to her, and she couldn't ignore them. So, after completing her scullery work, Gwendolyn often retreated to the castle gardens.

That day as she worked, she heard a lisping voice behind her. "Uckly."

Gwendolyn turned toward the voice. She smiled when she beheld Paul toddling through the garden. Attendants trailed behind him as he brushed chubby hands against flowers and cooed with pleasure.

Paul's eyes fastened upon Gwendolyn's face, and he pointed at her cheek. The dormant anger she'd tried to contain raised its head, and she couldn't help thinking, *The apple doesn't fall far from the tree.*

But Paul didn't scream or run from her. He smiled and lifted his hand in a wave. "Hurt?" he asked kindly, pointing at her cheek yet again.

Gwendolyn tentatively returned Paul's smile. "No, I'm not hurt." She suddenly felt shy. "You like flowers?" she asked.

Paul grinned at her. Then he frowned. "Uckly." He pointed at a weed-choked section of ground.

Gwendolyn nodded as understanding dawned. Chagrined, she said, "I've nearly reached them. I'll take the weeds away, and the flowers'll be pretty in a—"

Gwendolyn never understood what happened next. She only remembered that Paul crumpled to the ground. He wailed in pain, the cry splintering into an ululating howl. Gwendolyn screamed as Paul's face elongated. His garment ripped open. She lunged, clutching the child in her arms. Only he was no longer a child.

Attendants screamed, and someone grabbed Gwendolyn from behind, forcing her to relinquish her hold upon Paul.

"Witch," voices hissed. "He said she was ugly, and she cursed him."

Gwendolyn moaned as a familiar figure ran into the garden. Gustav's face crumpled as he beheld the chaos around him. Attendants advanced upon Gwendolyn, grabbing stones from the ground. She saw Gustav's eyes fill with tears as he turned to her, and she saw his lips move, forming a single question. "Why?"

Gwendolyn ran, sobbing with confusion. "I didn't do anything," she whispered to herself. But was that true? She hid in the scullery, listening to the panicked screams and the cries for her blood.

Footsteps sounded behind her, and she turned to stare into Claudio's haggard face. "What happened?" he demanded.

Gwendolyn shook, her mind spinning. "I-I don't know."

Claudio's face contorted with rage. "This evil is magic of the darkest kind. I know you, Gwendolyn. You'd never harm a child."

"What if the poisoned rose had long-term effects?" She thought of her whispered words on those days she'd arranged flowers before the wedding. *Her descendants will be as beastly as she is.* "I'm leaving here. I've hurt Gustav enough."

Before Claudio could speak, she walked away. As she did so, she whispered in a tear-choked voice, "I'm sorry."

CHAPTER SEVEN

*Y*ears passed, and Gwendolyn settled in a faraway village. She opened a florist's shop, keeping her face veiled to minimize customers' fear. Guilt burrowed inside her, a guilt she couldn't escape.

One day, a man had come to her shop to purchase flowers for a funeral. "Heard your flowers were the prettiest ever seen," he said. "Lovely flowers are needed for a duke's funeral."

Gwendolyn felt a shiver stroke her spine. "A duke?" she whispered.

She learned from the man that Gustav was dead. "Found in an apple orchard," the man told her. "Alongside his faithful butler. The butler had been mauled, and the duke had some wounds as well, although not life-threatening ones. But his face! Twisted into a mask of pain, it was. They'd both been left to die. The work of a demon."

When the man left, Gwendolyn retreated to the garden behind the shop. She sank to her knees, desperation clawing at her with ruthless fingers. She had to find help. There was no one to call to but Tecoptra. Even if he was a myth, he was all she had. She didn't even know how to ask, so she simply said, "Please." The pain-racked whisper tore from her.

A rustling sound filled her ears, and she looked up to see a white rose pulse with vibrant light. Its petals unfurled, opening wider than any rose she'd ever seen. She'd never seen this rose before. Shaking, Gwendolyn touched the flower, and fire exploded in her heart. The pain receded, replaced by a cleansing coolness.

A majestic voice filled the garden. *I have healed you. Now take me to where I can heal others. Well done, Gwendolyn.*

Gwendolyn trembled. "Who are you? How do you know my name?"

Do not be afraid. I am an emissary from Tecoptra. You unwittingly called down a curse upon Gustav's family, but now you seek to rectify your mistake. Tecoptra has sent me to help you. A rose cast the curse, so another rose will be instrumental in breaking it. Only the one who called down the curse could summon me. Now I must be taken to the castle so that I may complete my task. When a blind beauty requests a rose and a brother confronts a beast, I will die. Then the curse will be lifted.

Gwendolyn wept as she stared at the rose. She didn't speak, for simply saying thank you was inadequate. She would take the rose to Gustav's home and plant it there. It was a small gesture, but it was all she could do.

CHAPTER EIGHT

G wendolyn stood beside the castle gate two days later, the rose within her hand. How was she to enter? The rose shimmered, its light falling upon the gate.

This gate can only be opened from within, the rose told her. *But Tecoptra wills that I enter, so I shall do so.*

The gate slowly opened as the rose's light touched it. Shaking, Gwendolyn stepped onto the path and knelt, placing the rose within a clump of other white ones. As she did so, the rose vanished. Gwendolyn was frightened. Had she harmed it in some way?

Then the voice said, *I'll reveal myself in time.* The rose shone forth, winking at her. *Well done.*

Gwendolyn smiled and whispered, "Please bring healing and peace." The rose nodded, consenting to her words before vanishing yet again.

Gwendolyn left the castle grounds, her heart lighter than it had ever been. Perhaps she had finally done something good. She continued working in her shop, and she no longer wore the veil.

Meanwhile, the rose waited.

Part 2: The Bargain

Chapter Nine

*Y*ou really intend to marry him?" Jenna pounded bread dough with vicious fists.

Mirabel sighed wearily. "I just meant that if Reinhardt were to ask me, I'd consider it. I'm twenty-two. I can marry whom I choose."

Jenna sighed. "Reinhardt's old."

Mirabel laughed, tousling Jenna's hair. Jenna was such a romantic. "He's thirty-five. If I marry him, he'll be a help to Father."

Jenna snorted. "That's a ridiculous reason to marry someone! You can't be serious!"

"You're sixteen, Jenny. You should know by now that life isn't a fairy tale!" Mirabel spoke sharply. "Reinhardt helps us, and we must be grateful. Anyhow, he hasn't asked me, so there's no use discussing this."

"You marry someone for love," Jenna said. Glad that she'd had the last word, she lifted the pan of loaves, preparing to place them in the oven. Mirabel took the pan from her. "I can do it," Jenna sighed.

"You'll burn yourself." Mirabel spoke offhandedly, blushing when she saw Jenna flinch. "I'm sorry."

"It's all right." Jenna placed earthenware bowls on the table in the corner. She listened to the merry bubbling of simmering soup and inhaled the rich aroma of baking bread. "I hope Father brings back good news."

Mirabel smiled. "Me too. It would be wonderful to have a new dress. My old ones are worn to rags." After a moment, she said, "At least, if things aren't as good as the report says, your request shouldn't be hard to fulfill. Surely roses grow anywhere."

Jenna blushed. She thought of Father's merchant business. They had once possessed so many beautiful things. Then trouble had come upon the family. First, ships containing merchandise had been lost due to a storm. Then it was discovered that Father's bookkeeper had embezzled funds. Creditors came, demanding money. Soon the family was in desperate need. They had no choice but to dismiss the servants, and a new and more difficult way of life began.

Then the fire had occurred, a fire that Jenna didn't like to think about, for she had caused it. The family had been forced to move to a small cottage.

Jenna remembered the day when Mirabel had taken Mother's rosebushes to sell at market. Jenna had lashed out at her sister, calling her a heartless monster.

Mirabel listened to the tirade then said, her voice choked, "I miss her too, Jenny."

"You don't! No one does but me. I have to have the roses. I gave you the music box she gave me and the scarf she knitted with her own hands. I could hear the music and feel the scarf. Now you're taking her scent away too."

Mirabel sucked in her breath. "Don't you think it's hard for me? Do you think you're the only one in this family who's suffering?"

Jenna fell into her sister's arms, shaking uncontrollably. As always, her eyes burned. Mirabel rocked her to and fro.

"I'm horrid to you," Jenna whispered. "You're not really a monster."

Mirabel laughed through her tears. "Sometimes, I feel like a monster. I get so desperate. It's not easy doing Mother's job, you know. Can you be patient with me?"

After a long pause, Jenna nodded.

It was on that day that Mirabel started allowing Jenna to help her with simple household tasks. She even gave Jenna some freedom to walk in the apple orchard again. Years had passed since the day Jenna met the beast in the orchard, and he had never returned. Thus, Mirabel allowed the excursions. Jenna was immensely grateful, although she was no fool. She knew that Mirabel followed her at a discreet distance.

Jenna always remembered the strange creature with whom she'd conversed. He had been so like a boy. On her excursions to the orchard, she sat beneath the Tree with the Humped Back, eating peppermint drops and thinking of the mysterious meeting. She often wondered what had happened to the creature, and she regretted not knowing his name.

Now, Jenna said, "I know you think I'm silly, but I thought a rose would smell so lovely. We could put it on the table—"

A loud knock reverberated upon the cottage door. Jenna sighed. She knew that knock. "Should I let him in?"

Mirabel laughed. "Not with that frown on your face." She started toward the door and said over her shoulder, "I don't think you're silly, Jenny." She opened the door.

"Hello there, Miri." Reinhardt's musical baritone filled the cottage, a lovely voice of strength and compassion. He possessed the perfect voice for a physician. There was no denying his kindness. He had met the family when they moved to the cottage, bringing them a jar of honey as a gift. Of course, he'd offered to help them anyway he could, and now he was a frequent visitor. "Has Marcus arrived yet?"

"Not yet. We expected him back by now, but—"

"Understandable. Long way to the harbor. I imagine he stopped by the tavern. Good news warrants a celebration."

"Poppa wouldn't drink." Jenna spoke sharply, the words coming before she could stop them.

"How's my favorite patient?" Reinhardt's voice held a broad smile. "Been using the poultices for the pain like I told you?"

Jenna clenched her teeth. "They smell." She hated to admit it, but his poultices did relieve her pain. If Jenna was honest with herself, she disliked Reinhardt because he couldn't restore her sight.

"Bad smells make you well." Reinhardt laughed. Then his tone grew serious. "The fire destroyed your tear ducts. You must keep your eyes moist."

"I tell her that all the time." Mirabel sighed. "Do you want to stay for supper? I'm sure Father will arrive soon."

"If you'll have me. Brought you some wild basil. Nothing like it in tomato soup. Enhances the flavor."

"Thank you." Mirabel took the parcel Reinhardt proffered. "Was it a busy day?"

"Sickness never takes a holiday." He sighed and plopped onto a stool. "The usual colds and hypochondriac house calls, of course. There was a serious case of fever. The Willises' youngest boy."

Jenna stiffened, concern filling her heart. "Will he be all right?"

Reinhardt's tones were hopeful when he said, "I think I discovered it in time. And I almost forgot. Charlotte Willis gave me currant cake for payment. I brought you some."

Jenna had to smile at this. Reinhardt's sweet tooth was ferocious, almost as ferocious as her own. Sweets were such a rarity, and she couldn't remember the last time she'd tasted currant cake. "Thank you," she murmured.

The cottage door suddenly opened, and a figure stumbled inside. Jenna recognized Poppa's tread. He walked slower than usual.

"Poppa! What's wrong?" Mirabel cried. "You're so pale."

Reinhardt stood, his manner brusque. "Marcus, you must lie down."

When Poppa spoke, his voice was weak. "Don't fuss over me. I-I'm sorry, girls." He collapsed onto a chair. "It wasn't one of my ships."

"Don't worry, Poppa. We knew it might be wrong information," Mirabel said brightly. Despite her brave tone, Jenna heard the underlying disappointment. She herself didn't speak, for she didn't trust her voice. "You've had a hard journey. Supper'll be ready in a moment," Mirabel said.

Poppa spoke harshly. "Things will never be all right again. That journey cost me my life."

Mirabel gasped, and Jenna's stomach plummeted. Reinhardt said gruffly, "Don't overdramatize, my friend. Things will work out. They always do."

"Things are different now. I've bargained with a demon." Words poured from Poppa in a bitter stream.

CHAPTER TEN

M arcus always believed the best way to handle any situation was to face it head-on. So when he heard that the ship containing valuable merchandise had been located, he immediately resolved to see for himself. Then, when the report had proven false, he prepared to journey home and make do the best he could. He traveled a day and a night. The weather was becoming colder and colder the farther he walked. It was the beginning of spring, so cold nights were not unusual. What was unusual was the lack of familiar landmarks.

Marcus trudged along a path that, in the darkness, was not clearly defined. As he walked, torrential rain began to fall. What should he do now?

Then, before Marcus' eyes loomed a gate. It seemed to have appeared out of nowhere. He blinked in surprise. He approached it tentatively. The gate opened of its own accord. Marcus gasped, stepping back. Yet the rain pummeled him, and he needed directions. Perhaps the owners of this home would give him shelter.

Marcus stepped through the opened gate and onto a cobblestone walkway.

He gazed at the beautiful roses surrounding him. The garden was lush, and benches sat at convenient locations around it. A fountain chattered in the distance. A many-turreted castle shone just beyond the garden, a castle that gleamed with pearlescent light. As he approached the doors, they opened before him.

Marcus entered the gleaming foyer, listening to his echoing footsteps on the marble floor. The door slammed behind him with a reverberating boom.

"Hello?" Marcus called.

No answer came, and the vast halls rang with his voice. "I'm sorry for intruding. I'm lost and wondered if perhaps—"

"Who are you?" A thunderous voice caused Marcus to start violently. He scanned the area but could see no one. "State your business."

"I lost my way and need a place to stay. I can't see you. May I see who's addressing me?"

"No. Go up the stairs in the second corridor. You'll find a dining hall at the top of them. Supper awaits you there."

Marcus swallowed nervously. He thought it best to obey. He walked forward until he reached a spiral staircase. At the top of the stairs was an open door, through which wafted delicious smells. Marcus stepped across the threshold and blinked in shock. A round table was spread with a damask cloth. Upon the table sat platters of succulent meats, vegetables, and breads. A flagon of wine stood ready. His stomach growled with hunger, and he sat in the only chair at the table. He eyed the wine and wondered what would be the best way to indicate he preferred something else.

"Wine isn't to your liking, sir?" A voice emerged to his right. It seemed to be coming from atop the table.

Marcus jumped, dropping a roll he'd been slathering with butter. "Who said that?"

"Me, of course."

Marcus turned his head, his eyes fastening onto the gleaming brass of a candelabra. The candles winked on and off as if they were laughing. Marcus placed his hand to his head. "I'm dreaming."

"Sorry, chap. Didn't think to bring other drinks. Just ask for what you want."

"You're a candelabra. You're speaking to me." Marcus' head swam.

"Excellent observation, my good man. Actually, I'm a servant, not a mere object. Now, do you want tea? Or we have some excellent raspberry cordial."

If he played along, he'd awaken faster. At least, Marcus hoped this was the case. "I haven't had raspberry cordial since I was a boy," he said. "I'll have that, please."

He watched in shock as a glass bottle suddenly appeared before his eyes. It hovered in the air just above the table. The candles winked again.

"You'll have to pour it, chap. Liquid and flame, you know."

Marcus reached out his hand and touched the bottle. It was solid. Suddenly, he laughed. He hadn't laughed in so long. He began to eat. Everything was cooked to perfection, and the cordial was light and sweet.

When Marcus finished eating, the candelabra jumped from the table and hovered in the doorway, blinking on and off in an expectant manner. "I'll show you to your room."

Marcus followed the flickering candles down several corridors to a chamber with a large four-poster bed. He suddenly realized how tired he was. The bed linens were turned down, and the moment that Marcus sank into the mattress' embrace, he fell into a deep slumber.

The next morning, the same candelabra awakened Marcus and showed him to the dining hall. After a sumptuous breakfast, he prepared to leave. Feeling foolish for talking to candlesticks (apparently he wasn't dreaming after all), Marcus asked, "How might I thank my host? I haven't seen him. Last night, he stayed in the shadows, and—"

"He did what any self-respecting host would do. No need to thank him." The candelabra led Marcus to the castle door. It opened, and Marcus stepped outside into brilliant sunlight.

Dew glimmered on the pathway, making the roses sparkle like rubies and pearls. As Marcus walked toward the gate, he couldn't help admiring them. Images of Jenna filled his mind. She'd asked that he bring her a single rose. All he was bringing home was sorrow. Surely he could bring home some beauty as well. As he surveyed the roses, he saw a most unusual one. The rose shimmered with rainbow hues of brilliance. He held out his hand, ready to pluck the flower.

Footfalls erupted behind him, and something pushed against him—a large, angry something. Marcus had just enough time to glimpse a gaping mouth and bloodshot eyes before falling to his knees. He felt something sharp press against his shoulder.

"Is this proper payment for my hospitality?" The thunderous voice made the marrow in Marcus' bones congeal. The voice continued, "I give you lodging and feed you from my own larder. In return, you steal from me? For this transgression, you must die."

"I meant no harm. Please have mercy," Marcus whispered.

"And would you show mercy to someone who robbed you?" The voice was still angry, but there was an underlying note of curiosity.

Marcus swallowed. "I-I don't know," he finally admitted.

"Then I see no reason to honor your request." The speaker stepped in front of Marcus.

A monster stood before him, a towering beast with the body of a wolf and the head of a deer. A colossal pair of antlers jutted from the beast's head. They were crowned with many sharp points. Yet it was the face that struck terror into Marcus' heart. It was twisted into a hideous scowl, and the sagging left cheek bore a crimson-hued mark upon it. The beast lowered his head, preparing to impale Marcus with his antlers. Then something in his protruding eyes changed, and he spoke harshly, the words tumbling out in a rush.

"Your face. It bears a strong resemblance to—do you have a daughter who cannot see?"

Marcus blinked. "Y-yes," he stammered. "How did you know?" Then the memories came to him. Marcus' heart plummeted. "You're the beast that tried to attack my—"

"I'd advise you to stop talking." The beast's tone was deadly. "You may go. In a month's time, you will return to me and suffer my wrath. If your daughter chooses to come in your place, I'll accept her instead. But she must come willingly."

Knives thrust themselves into Marcus' heart. "I'll not bargain with the likes of you."

"Would you rather die here and now? Either you come back, or I'll make you return. I'll tell my friends, and they'll summon a zephyr to collect you." He shifted his gaze to the

45

roses. "I'm giving you a chance to tell your family goodbye, so I'd take advantage of it if I were you."

Marcus had no choice but to obey. He rose and turned toward the castle gate. As he did so, his eyes alighted upon the spot where the rainbow-hued rose had stood. It was no longer there. Had it all been a trap? "I'll return," he whispered.

"Very well. I've instructed the roses to call forth a zephyr to take you home."

Marcus tried to comprehend what the beast might mean, but there wasn't time, for a gentle breeze wrapped itself around him, and he felt himself being lifted into the air.

Rustling voices repeatedly whispered one word: *Sleep*.

Marcus couldn't resist and sank into a heavy slumber.

When he awoke, he found himself in the apple orchard his daughters loved so much. Weeping, he trudged homeward.

CHAPTER ELEVEN

Marcus completed his story, his eyes brimming with tears. Jenna's head swam in shock.

Reinhardt was the first to speak. "If this extraordinary story is true, then we must kill that fiend."

"That's the problem. I don't know where that demon's den is." Marcus stared at his daughters' stricken faces and Reinhardt's incredulous one. "Think I'm mad if you want, Reinhardt. I know what I saw and heard. I'll leave in a month, and I'm sure I'll find the castle again."

"I don't think you're mad, Marcus." Reinhardt spoke softly, his voice trembling. "I myself have seen . . ." His voice trailed away.

Jenna spoke, her voice taut. "He said he'd accept me if I went willingly, and I'll do just that."

"Don't say such things, Jenna," Mirabel snapped.

"It's my fault Poppa's in trouble. I asked for the rose."

"You couldn't have known this would happen. If it's true, then I'll go," Mirabel said.

"Don't you understand? I can't see. That's why he wants me to come. I won't run away because his looks won't frighten me."

Marcus spoke with finality. "This discussion is pointless. I'm going back there."

Jenna said nothing more then, for she knew her words would profit little.

On the night before Poppa was supposed to leave, she stole from the cottage, her guidance tool in hand. She'd go to the apple orchard first, just for one last visit with the humpbacked tree. From there, she didn't know what to do, but if Poppa had found the castle, she felt certain she would too.

Crickets serenaded Jenna as she stealthily crept through the orchard. She reached her tree, pausing to caress its rough bark. Through all these years, it still stood strong. "I'll miss you," she whispered.

"What're you doing?"

Jenna's stomach clenched at Mirabel's taut voice. She sighed and turned from the tree. "Why must you always interfere, Miri?"

"Are you mad? Do you think I didn't know your intentions? Confound it, Jenny!"

"I have to do this," Jenna said. "You can't stop me."

"Yes, I can."

"You're saying you want Poppa to die?" Jenna hated asking the question. Yet words poured from her in brittle fragments. "I won't let Poppa die. I killed Mother—"

Mirabel slapped her, a stinging blow that caused Jenna to cry out. The slap didn't hurt, but the betrayal did. Mirabel had never struck her.

"Stop this!" Mirabel hissed. "You didn't kill Mother. How dare you say such a thing?"

"I did! She told me to stir the soup, and I ran from the house, leaving the fire burning. I told her I hated her. I was so angry." Jenna trembled, her eyes burning worse than ever. She swallowed down the sadness, feeling it scorch her throat. She abruptly turned and began walking away, paying no heed to Mirabel's frantic cries. Even when

Mirabel grabbed at her, she shrank from her grasp and continued doggedly onward.

It was then that she heard a low, gentle whisper. "Jenna."

She blinked, trying to determine where the voice was coming from. "Hello?"

"I'll help you. Just stop walking so that the zephyr might lift you."

Jenna shuddered. The voice was strange, a rustling voice that did not sound human. She felt a gentle touch upon her back, and the ground shifted beneath her. Suddenly, she was lifted into the air, and a breeze stroked her face. The breeze carried the fragrance of apples. "Sleep," the voice whispered. "When you awaken, he'll be near you."

Jenna struggled against the breeze. Her heart pounded with terror. Then the voice spoke again. "Tecoptra bade me help you. I remember the day the castle-dweller bade me frighten you. Afterward, I wept with remorse, as did he. Now I can make amends."

Jenna swallowed. "You're the Tree with the Humped Back. You can speak?"

Rustling laughter surrounded her. "Of course, although I don't usually speak your language. Tecoptra has enabled me to do so. Sleep now. I've instructed the zephyr to carry you to the castle."

Jenna felt so tired. She sank into the apple-scented embrace of the breeze and slept.

CHAPTER TWELVE

Mirabel gasped as she observed the impossible. The apple tree moved of its own accord, its branches rustling repeatedly. She saw Jenna standing stock-still, and although Mirabel tried to go to her, her feet wouldn't budge. A gentle breeze blew, and Jenna was lifted into the air, immediately vanishing from sight.

Mirabel screamed and began to run. Yet how could one catch the wind? She wept hysterically, her heart breaking in two.

"Miri? What's wrong?" A voice rang behind her, and she spun around, crying in relief as she saw Reinhardt entering the orchard.

"It's Jenna. She's been taken by sorcery." Trembling, she pointed at the tree, a searing anger filling her heart. "It's this tree's doing. I-I must—"

"Calm down!" Reinhardt spoke sharply, reaching for her hand. His face wore a concerned frown. "I'll take you home."

"No. I have to find Jenna."

Reinhardt took her hand. "You can't abandon Marcus. Just come with me, and we'll determine what to do." He led Mirabel from the orchard and to the cottage. When he opened the door, he saw that the room was empty. "Jenna left to find the castle. Marcus has gone after her, hasn't he?" he asked sharply.

"I don't know. He was asleep when I left. I followed her—"

"You must have something to settle your nerves." Reinhardt reached into the cloth bag he always carried. He murmured, "It's fortunate a doctor never gets any rest. Otherwise, I wouldn't have found you. I was visiting the Willis boy." He drew a glass bottle from the bag and uncorked it. The scent of raspberries filled the cottage. "Sit down. This cordial will help."

Mirabel sank onto the cot in the corner of the room. Reinhardt placed the bottle into her hand. "Drink it all. Doctor's orders."

Mirabel accepted the drink, raising her eyebrows in surprise at the heady taste. "It's delicious," she said.

Reinhardt smiled. "Now, tell me everything." He sat on the stool beside the cot, waiting expectantly.

Mirabel began her story, her voice trembling. As she spoke, she felt soft fingers of fatigue caress her mind, and she stumbled over her words. Her eyes began to close, and though she fought against sleep, it claimed her with vicious insistence.

Reinhardt rose. When he spoke, his voice was very gentle. "Don't worry, Miri. I'll take care of everything. Sleep, lovely one. Sleep and forget your sorrow as I cannot."

He bent and tenderly stroked her sleep-slackened cheek. "I had to do it, Miri. You'd have followed me otherwise. There'll be no lasting effects. You know I'd never harm you." He turned and left the cottage.

Reinhardt stood before the humpbacked apple tree. He caressed its bark, his heart hammering with fear and anticipation. "Take me there as you did the girl," he whispered.

"You're a very sad man." The tree rustled gently, sending forth the gift of its fragrance. "Why do you hate him so?"

Reinhardt's face contorted. "Obey me this instant."

"You've changed so much, master." The tree's branches trembled with compassion. "I remember when you were a boy. You and the young girl would sit beneath my branches and read stories to each other. I remember how you'd pretend to be a knight. You'd rescue her from dragons and trolls. When you grew older, I gave you blossoms and leaves. The young woman was quite fond of apple-scented soap, wasn't she?"

Reinhardt reached into his bag, withdrawing a metal scalpel. His face flushed with rage. "Do you know how it feels to watch someone you love wasting away? You try every medicine known and some not known, yet nothing helps. You hold your sister in your arms as she dies. You dare remind me of my failure?"

He plunged the scalpel into the tree's heart. The tree writhed, a harrowing scream filling the air. Sap bled from the hole, and Reinhardt wept as he watched.

"I cannot pass through that confounded castle gate. It won't open to me." His face crumpled. "Curse paltry magic! If I were an enchanter, I could force you to obey me as I could force all these trees, but I must address each of you individually. Why did you send a defenseless girl into danger? You're a fool!"

Reinhardt patted the tree's trunk. When he spoke again, his voice was gentle. "Perhaps you know no better. I can mend your wound. It's your decision. Help me, and I'll help you."

"The beast means the girl no harm. Tecoptra willed that she go to the castle. Things aren't always what they seem, master," the tree whispered.

Reinhardt's features hardened. "I must find a friend and take him home. I'll return to you, and when I do, I advise you to obey my command. You know nothing. I've seen with my own eyes what that fiend is capable of."

"You're a Flower Master, and a strong one at that. Your anger compels me to obey you. Yet Tecoptra is my true master. I know full well what the beast can do, but I've done things as well. Incidentally, my brothers and sisters will not obey you either. Not after this betrayal." His branches rustled sadly.

Reinhardt flinched and averted his gaze. "Your pain will increase, and your death will come much slower than you think."

He turned away, his mind spinning. He'd committed a heinous act, and he regretted it. Even so, he was desperate. If the tree had just listened to reason! He trudged through the orchard. Now to find Marcus. He'd take him home and try to formulate another plan. No one could pass through that castle gate unless the monster willed that they do so. Reinhardt knew this from experience. Yet he would do everything in his power to help his friend. He had failed others in the past. He would not fail now.

CHAPTER THIRTEEN

J enna awoke to the sound of clinking cutlery. She lay upon soft linen. The scent of roses wafted around her.

"Awake, are you?" A reverberating voice rumbled, and Jenna shrank from its harsh timbre. "I brought you some peppermint tea."

Jenna swallowed. "Thank you," she whispered.

The voice was amused when it said, "Don't waste time thanking me. Just answer this one question: Did you come willingly? I found you on my morning walk. You lay on a bench in the garden. I assume the roses let you in."

Jenna blinked. "I came willingly," she said. "And when someone does something nice for someone else, they should be thanked. It's only polite."

The beast laughed, a rumbling sound that resembled a lion's roar. "Politeness is irrelevant here. I want no favors."

Jenna sat up, and a cup of tea was placed in her hand. She sipped it gratefully. "I don't want favors, either. I want to apologize for what happened that day. I tried to stop them from hurting you, but—"

"Hurting me?" The beast spoke harshly. "What're you talking about?"

"Why, the day in the apple orchard, of course. I'm not sure what happened. Poppa grabbed me, and I heard arrows flying. I've never forgotten it. How did you escape?"

"Apple orchard? I've never left these grounds."

Jenna's mind reeled in confusion. "I don't understand. How do you remember me, then? How did you know I couldn't see?"

"Because of my dream." He spoke softly, or as softly as such a voice could speak. "It's a recurring dream I've had ever since I was a boy. I see a girl who cannot see me. She meets me in an apple orchard, and we talk. She never runs away, for she has no cause for fear." He laughed bitterly. "It's such a relief to talk to someone, even in a dream. As we converse, we partake of peppermint drops. If I'm not dreaming of you, then the girl has your face."

The Tree with the Humped Back filled Jenna's mind. After a moment, she told her story of the apple orchard from the beginning, not even omitting the portion where he had caused her to fall.

When she finished speaking, the beast whispered, his voice shaking, "I always suspected you were real. The dream was so vivid. Yet I never dared hope. I'm going to stand beside the bed, and I want you to touch me. You cannot see, but that doesn't mean you shouldn't know what I am."

Jenna trembled, but she held out her hand expectantly. She heard the scrape of large paws upon marble, and a gigantic head came to rest against her palm. Her fingers groped a long muzzle, a sagging left cheek with jagged fur, and protruding eyes. Then she encountered a pair of branching antlers, their multiple points sharp as thorns.

Beneath her hand, the creature shook, his body tense. "The antlers could gore you in an instant," he said matter-of-factly. "Are you willing to risk staying here?"

Jenna shuddered. She couldn't help it. At the same time, she suddenly realized that the antlers felt familiar. In fact, she recalled how something sharp had brushed her hand the day she'd fallen from the tree. She whispered, "I'm willing to stay with you."

After a long silence, the beast said, "I'll leave you now. Tonight, will you join me for supper?"

"Yes," Jenna said. She listened as the beast strode to the door. Quickly, she asked, "Please, sir. What should I call you?"

He laughed that harsh laugh again, a sound of bitter amusement. "Beast will suffice."

"No." Jenna trembled at her daring, but the refusal had already been spoken. "I meant, what's your name?"

"It's Beast. You'll call me that, for it's what I am."

"The villagers call me Blind. It's a title that limits me. I'm not calling you by a mere title. My name's Jenna. If you won't tell me your name, then I won't call you anything. Then what kind of conversations would we have?"

"Am I master here or not?" the beast growled angrily. Then he said, "My name is Paul." He stormed from the room before Jenna could say anything else.

Jenna rose from the bed and groped around the chamber. Opening a massive wardrobe door, she brushed her hands along an array of gowns and night apparel. *Mirabel would love these clothes*, she thought.

"Can I help, my lady?" A young, female voice filled the room, and Jenna started, for she hadn't heard the door open.

"I'm fine, thank you."

"I can get you any gown you prefer. Lots of varying colors. I think a plum gown would be best."

Although Jenna strained her ears, she heard no footfall or rustling garment. Moreover, the voice seemed to be issuing from the wardrobe through which her hands were rummaging. "What's your name? May I shake your hand?"

The voice laughed. "I apologize, my lady. I have no hand for you to shake. Not anymore." The voice was suddenly sad.

Jenna swallowed nervously. Poppa's story of the candelabra. It was true. "You're a wardrobe?"

"Didn't I hear you tell the master you wouldn't answer to titles? Nor shall I. My name's Betsy. Do you want a gown? If not, kindly close these confounded doors. I was trying to sleep."

Jenna laughed. "You choose the gown, please. I don't know what to suggest. May I ask how you were enchanted?"

Betsy sighed, and garments rustled upon hooks. Then Jenna felt a gown as soft as gossamer land within her hands, a garment with teardrop-shaped beads upon its collar.

"Seed pearls," Betsy murmured, "set against plum and rose silk. To answer your question, Claudio caused my enchantment to happen. He claimed to be an amateur enchanter. I, however, disagree." She laughed. "I'm in this state, aren't I? That's not the work of a novice."

Jenna fingered the brilliant gown she held, her mind spinning in confusion. "Who was Claudio? Was he evil?"

"Evil? My, no! Claudio sought to protect his charges at all costs. He was the head servant. A very kind man who would do anything for anyone. Then—"

Betsy's voice broke, but she finally said, "It was the day of Paul's fifteenth birthday. When I brought him his tea, he rushed at me like a madman, demanding to leave the grounds. He howled, charging from the room. I've never heard such pitiful screams."

Betsy related how the duke had been wounded when he tried to prevent Paul from leaving the grounds. Claudio had stepped between father and son as they battled.

"Claudio was so old," Betsy whispered, "so very frail. He was killed. As he lay dying, he said, 'I've done all I can, Gustav. I've ensured that the servants will not leave, as they will desire to help you, and the roses will help too.' When he died, the changes came upon us."

Jenna shivered. "As he died, Claudio changed the servants into objects?"

"Yes, my lady. Claudio didn't realize that the enchantment was so strong. The magic misinterpreted his directions and made certain the servants would stay, no matter what. Duke Gustav died soon after that day. No one quite knows how, but he was terribly upset about Claudio's death. Many of us think the distress acted upon his heart. Paul has never sought to leave the castle again."

Jenna felt sadness grip her heart. She knew what it was like to be confined. She loved her family and would do anything for them, yet she also battled with anger against them. So wasn't she as much of a beast as Paul? She knew she couldn't hide in this room. She resolved to make the most of her time at the castle.

CHAPTER FOURTEEN

The rest of the day was spent exploring the gigantic castle. Jenna met the candelabra, whose name was Lucian. She laughed when she heard the clinking of his footsteps following her down corridors.

"I know you don't need light, miss," Lucian said once, "but it's such a treat having a human here. Is it permissible for me to walk with you occasionally?"

Jenna smiled. "Of course." She turned down one more corridor, her nose suddenly filling with the wonderful scent of leather-bound books. She opened a door and stepped into a room that held the fragrance of knowledge. *A library,* she thought with longing. She began shuffling along numerous bookshelves, stroking dusty spines. She took a book from a shelf and rifled through its pages, delighting in the brusque conversation of rustling paper.

"Could you once see?" The reverberating voice spoke behind her, and Jenna jumped, dropping the book. "I didn't mean to frighten you." Paul's voice was heavy with weary regret.

"I didn't hear you come in," Jenna said.

"You were absorbed. It's teatime. I always take tea in the library. Would you like some?"

"Yes, please," Jenna murmured. She followed Paul's reverberating footsteps until she reached a table. She sat within a wicker chair. A tea tray containing cucumber and pâté sandwiches and chocolate cake sat upon the table before her.

Jenna's stomach growled. She remembered lavish teas from happier times, and she reveled in the bounty before her. As she ate, she said, "You asked if I could once see. Yes, I could, but I was burned in a fire." She swallowed and blinked rapidly. "Mother was killed." She placed her fork onto her plate, her appetite suddenly gone.

"What happened?" Paul's voice was gentle.

Jenna sat down her cup, listening to it rattle upon its saucer. "They always say that I didn't do it, but I know what happened." Her hands began to shake.

"Tell me."

"You wouldn't understand."

"I think I would!" Paul spoke harshly, and Jenna trembled. She thought of Betsy's story.

"I was twelve," Jenna said. "It was fall festival time, and there was to be a dance. I wanted to go. Mother said she needed help and that I couldn't go. We'd dismissed our servants, and that meant extra work for all of us. It's funny, because I didn't really care about the dance. I was angry about our misfortune.

"I told Mother I hated her. I ran from the house, forgetting that I had soup simmering on the hearth. Mother ran after me, but I hid in the woods, listening to her search for me. I don't know how long I stayed there, but suddenly I saw a plume of smoke coming from our house. I remember hearing Mother scream as I ran toward the house. When I burst into the clearing, our home was ablaze, and she was inside, trying to put out the flames. I rushed inside to help her and felt the heat surround me, but she tried to shove me back outside. Then the roof collapsed, and I don't remember anything more.

"I must have fainted, because when I woke up, I learned that Mother had died. She'd pushed me to safety, but she'd been crushed by debris when a portion of the house collapsed. I-I killed my own—" Jenna stopped speaking, only then realizing how hard she was breathing.

"There's a difference between deliberately killing and doing so by accident," Paul said. "You left her, but then you came back."

"That doesn't change anything. She's dead." Jenna stood and turned from the table. "Tea's meant to be a peaceful meal, and I've spoiled it for you. I'm sorry."

The silence seemed exceedingly heavy, and then Paul spoke, his voice shaking. "When I killed Claudio, I was so frightened. I remember awakening on my fifteenth birthday, and I somehow knew that I was being held prisoner here. Father wouldn't let me leave, and we struggled. Then Claudio stepped between us. 'Let him go, master,' Claudio kept saying. 'I'll follow him.' But Father wouldn't listen."

Paul's voice broke, and a whimper escaped his throat. "I struck blindly with my antlers, and Claudio fell. I remember screaming at Father, telling him it was all his fault. Father turned away from me and reentered the castle. Two days later, he was walking in these gardens. I was watching from an upstairs window and saw him clutch his chest and collapse. I ran into the garden and saw that he was lying so still. His face was twisted with pain.

"He raised his head and looked me in the eyes. It was the first time he'd ever looked at me directly. 'Monster,' he gasped, his words barely audible. 'They will call you a monster. People will try to kill you. You must promise me you'll never leave here.' I knew that Father was right, but before I could tell him that I would obey him, he was dead.

"I was so terrified! The servants had been transformed, and I was alone. I pleaded for someone to help me. The roses sang me to sleep, and when I awoke, Father's body was gone. I hid in the castle, resolving never to leave. Yet I couldn't banish thoughts of the roses from my mind, so I continued tending them daily."

Jenna trembled. "You didn't have to tell me that."

"Yes, I did. I want you to know that I understand. Both our parents are dead, and we each have experienced guilt."

Jenna sucked in her breath. She felt tired but oddly relieved, almost as if a stone had been lifted from her chest. Even so, she hadn't meant to cause Paul pain. Telling his story had obviously been hard for him, as difficult as telling hers had been for her. She shuffled toward the library door.

"I observed you with the books." Paul spoke urgently, a desperate cry in his voice. "What types of books do you like the best?"

Jenna turned and slowly sat back down. "Fairy tales. I know I'm too old for them, but I like stories where evil is vanquished. Mirabel's always reminding me that life isn't a fairy tale. I know that, of course, but it's so nice to dream. Those stories give me hope."

Paul was silent for a time. Then he murmured, "I like them too, even if they're wishful thinking. I think I can help you." He stood and walked to a shelf. Jenna heard a peculiar sound, the sound of scratching against paper. Then Paul returned. "I'm placing this paper in front of you. Do you remember what letters look like?"

"I think so."

"It's just an idea. Touch the paper."

Her hands trembling, Jenna ran her fingers along the paper. It bore claw marks in the exact shape of letters. She traced the first letter, feeling a circle beneath her fingers.

O, she thought. Then she traced the second letter, two vertical lines with a diagonal one in the center of them. *N*. Then a half-circle. *C*. Then a vertical line with three horizontal ones jutting to the right of it. *E*.

Jenna gasped with joy. It was as if a fountain had been unstopped. Cleansing coolness filled her. Even if this feeling did not last, the sadness was momentarily gone. She read four of the most beautiful words ever written: "Once upon a time." That was all Paul had written, but it was enough.

"Thank you," she whispered.

Paul laughed as he had done so often before, but the sound was not as bitter as usual. "You're welcome," he said.

CHAPTER FIFTEEN

*e*ach day was a new adventure. Jenna walked with Paul in the garden, and they spent much time in the library. With Jenna's help, Paul refined his system so that she could read. She did not read quickly, and transcribing was tedious work, but Jenna relished the times she and Paul held copies of the same story in their hands. They'd read together and travel to distant lands.

Each night, they partook of sumptuous meals. The first time Jenna had expressed a longing for Peppermint Surprise, a dessert that Mirabel used to make, she'd been shocked to find a large dish of the fragrant dessert in front of her. Tentatively, she had tasted the dessert, delighting in the melting marshmallows, whipped cream, and brittle fragments of refreshing mint candy. She remembered Poppa's story of the cordial bottle that had magically appeared. Paul told her that Claudio had ensured that food and drink of any kind would always be available.

After the meals, Paul and Jenna retired to a lavish music room. They were treated to magnificent concerts. The violins, cellos, trumpets, and clarinets played of their own accord, as did the grand piano.

One night, they even danced together. This attempt was rather dismal, for they both had two left feet, but the experience was worthwhile. Before long, a month had passed.

Each night before retiring to their bedchambers, Paul asked Jenna the same questions: "Do you want to stay here? Are you happy with me?"

Jenna always answered in the affirmative, but over time, her answer to the first question was hesitant. Paul noticed this, of course.

One night, Paul said, "You cannot pretend with me. Tell me what is wrong."

"I want to see my father and sister again. I miss them so much," Jenna whispered.

Paul moved closer to her. His voice was choked when he said, "The night your father came here, I was terrified. The roses later told me they felt sorry for him. That's why they let him in. I allowed him to stay simply to hear another human voice. The next morning, I saw him reach toward my friends. He meant to take one away from me. I was furious and frightened. When I saw his face for the first time, I was shocked. There are gaps in my memory, times I cannot reclaim. Like I told you, my dream of you was so real. I made that bargain with your father because I was so lonely. You've filled my heart with such joy, Jenna. I can't bear for you to leave me."

"You asked the question, and I answered honestly. I won't leave you," Jenna said. The sadness that had been sleeping in her heart suddenly awoke.

There was a long silence. Then Paul said, "And yet, if you don't leave here, you'll be miserable." Jenna heard him suck in his breath, and when he spoke again, his voice was sharp. "You'll leave tomorrow."

"What?"

"You heard me." He turned abruptly and stormed from the room.

Jenna trudged to her bedchamber. She lay down and succumbed to the sadness, feeling it invade her mind. She longed to go home, yet she also longed to stay with Paul. Gradually, she sank into a fitful sleep.

PART THREE: THE CONFRONTATION

CHAPTER SIXTEEN

T he cottage walls pulsed with ominous silence. Poppa lay still as death. Mirabel bent over him, running a damp cloth across his fevered brow. Poppa had been sick for three weeks, and the fever wouldn't break. Reinhardt had brought Poppa home the night Jenna had left. For the first week of Jenna's absence, Poppa had journeyed far each day, determined to find her. Every night, he returned to the cottage, despair enshrouding him. The fever had come upon him suddenly and relentlessly.

Mirabel sobbed. If only Jenna were here. Mirabel knew that Poppa's illness wasn't simply physical. It was the result of a broken heart.

Mirabel glanced around the cottage. Her eyes alighted upon Reinhardt's cloth bag. He'd gone to retrieve more water and would return shortly. Reinhardt had tried so many medicines, seeking something to break the fever. Was it possible Mirabel could find something herself? She retrieved the bag, peering inside at boxes and bottles.

"What're you doing?"

Mirabel started and turned, staring into Reinhardt's fatigued face. She hadn't heard him enter.

"I'm trying to find something to help him. You aren't helping—" Mirabel's voice broke, and tears coursed down her cheeks. "I didn't mean that. I-I'm sorry."

Reinhardt took the bag from Mirabel's hand. "I'm doing all I can, Miri."

Mirabel nodded. "I don't know what I'd do without you. Isn't there any hope? Be honest with me." Her face crumpled with pain.

Reinhardt drew Mirabel into his arms. "As long as the heart beats, there is hope, Miri. Yet I fear that Marcus' illness stems from despair. If a person loses the will to live—" His voice trailed away, and his features hardened. "Rest assured that if I cannot save Marcus, I can at least avenge his death, and Jenna's as well. I won't allow that monster to hurt anyone else, and I'll do all I can to protect you."

He ran his fingers through Mirabel's chestnut hair and gently kissed her lips. As he felt her respond, euphoria filled him. They were so alike, kindred spirits fighting against an unjust world. He drew her closer. "You fill me with such joy," he breathed.

Mirabel moaned, disentangling herself from his embrace. She shook, her knees as weak as water. His kiss was the stuff of fairy tales, the kiss of an ardent prince. It was wonderful, and yet it was terrifying. She longed to let him hold her, but if she did, she knew where it would lead. Her eyes strayed to Poppa's sleeping form.

"Please don't," she whispered.

Reinhardt blinked as if awakening from a dream. Trembling, he stepped away from her. "Forgive me," he whispered. "I'll find that demon tonight. I'll kill him."

Miles away in Paul's castle, Jenna awoke. She heard screaming. The screams were her own.

CHAPTER SEVENTEEN

The door of Jenna's chamber banged open, and Paul rushed in. His voice rumbled with concern when he asked, "What's wrong?"

The dream came pouring out, and Jenna whispered, "Poppa's sick. He may be dying."

There was a long silence, and finally Paul said, "The man could already be near here. Dreams are not bound by time. You have to leave here. The flowers will carry you home. I'll ensure your safety."

"No," Jenna said. "I can't leave you. You're in danger."

"You'll leave here." Paul's tone was harsh. "And you'll leave now." He stepped to her side. "I'm taking you to the rose garden. You'll allow the flowers to put you to sleep. They'll summon a zephyr to carry you home."

Jenna's eyes flooded with tears. "I can't leave you, yet I can't allow Poppa to die."

Paul sucked in his breath. He didn't speak, for he didn't trust his voice. He simply led Jenna from her chamber to the gardens.

Outside, the air was redolent with the clean scent of newly fallen rain. Jenna and Paul stood together upon the cobblestoned path. "Will you remember me?" Paul whispered.

"Of course I will. I'll return as soon as I can. I promise."

Paul bent his head, and Jenna felt his antlers gently brush her palm. Then he stepped away from her, and she heard the roses begin to sing sleep into her veins. A gentle breeze began to blow. As Jenna was lifted into the air, the castle gate opened of its own accord.

Desperately, she said, "You could come with me." Then she was carried through the gate. Before drifting into sleep, she felt something caress her hair, but her mind was so heavy with sorrow, she thought nothing of it.

Paul watched Jenna go. A howl of desolation escaped him. Then he was running toward the gate, desperate for a final glimpse of the one he loved. She wouldn't return. Why would she?

As Paul stepped through the gate, he felt a biting pain slice into his shoulder. He howled and crumpled to the ground. A hand slammed against his shoulder, causing percussive vibrations of agony to course through his entire body. Paul raised his head, and a flushed-faced man sneered down at him. In the man's hand was clutched a bloodstained butcher knife.

"I knew if I was patient, the gate would open. And here you are, finally emerging into the wide world." The man aimed a kick at Paul's form, sending him back through the gate. When Reinhardt stepped inside, the gate slammed shut.

CHAPTER EIGHTEEN

The zephyr deposited Jenna by the cottage door, and she rushed inside. Mirabel gasped in shock and ran to her sister, enfolding her in her embrace. "Jenny! You escaped!" She was shaking.

Jenna hurried to Poppa's cot. She felt his forehead, gasping at how hot it was. As she knelt down, her disheveled hair brushed against his face. She wept with pain. "We must find help," Jenna said.

"Reinhardt's been giving him medicine, but nothing's helping. He left two days ago to find that monster and kill him."

Jenna nodded and quickly told Mirabel her dream. "I must go back to the orchard. The Tree with the Humped Back transported me to the castle. I think he'll do it again."

Mirabel stepped to Jenna's side. "Why would you go back there?" she asked harshly. "Why must you leave me again? That demon has bewitched you."

Jenna swallowed. "Paul's kind, Miri. He let me go. I can't let him be hurt."

"Paul?" Mirabel's voice held a smile, the first one in days. "You're the only person I know who would ask a beast its name, Jenny." She sighed. "I've always tried to protect you, yet you've never needed it. Poppa can't be left. I'll stay with him." She drew a shuddering breath. "Go if you must."

Jenna embraced Mirabel tightly. "I don't always show it, but I love you, Miri." She kissed her sister and ran from the house.

It was only then that Mirabel noticed something peculiar. Poppa was stirring on the cot. She ran to his side and stroked his forehead. It was cool to her touch. Weeping with joy, Mirabel gaped as a rainbow-hued rose petal fluttered from Poppa's face to the ground.

CHAPTER NINETEEN

Reinhardt had not lied, for dying was indeed painful. The Tree with the Humped Back trembled in agony. His frame buckled, and a single cry issued from his rustling branches. "Please, Tecoptra."

A breeze caressed his leaves. *Courageous one, I am sending help.*

It was that moment that Jenna approached. The Tree with the Humped Back recognized her shuffling gait. His heart melted when he felt her familiar touch, but he wept, for he was too weak to help her.

Jenna gasped when her groping fingers felt the hole in her tree's side. Sticky sap coated her fingers. She shuddered. What was going on?

At that moment, a stoop-shouldered woman entered the orchard. She scanned the area around her, the crimson mark upon her cheek gleaming more lividly than ever. Gwendolyn knew the cry of a tree in distress. It had awakened her from sleep, and she'd journeyed far to find its source.

She approached the tree, gasping when she saw its mangled frame. "Tecoptra help me," she whispered. She saw a young girl with a scarred face and disheveled black hair. The girl was standing beside the tree, and she was shaking.

Compassion filled Gwendolyn's heart. "Perhaps I can help him, miss."

She placed her hand upon the tree's bleeding heart. Its life's blood pulsed against her fingers. She began speaking words of encouragement. She smiled as she felt the ebbing blood cease. When she drew her hand away, the wound was gone. Only a cross-shaped scar remained.

The tree wept with joy, his branches rustling thanks.

Gwendolyn smiled and addressed Jenna. "He'll be all right now."

Jenna gasped, fingering the scar where the hole had been. "Please, ma'am. I don't know who you are, but I need help." She told her story hastily. She knew this woman would think her mad, but she was desperate. "I must return to the castle. Paul needs me."

Gwendolyn stared at the young woman. "The curse will be lifted when a blind beauty requests a rose and a brother confronts a beast," she whispered to herself. She remembered how the kitchen workers often talked of the physicians who came to examine Sauda.

One maid had talked of a handsome young man. " 'E gives 'er tea and cordial. 'E won't leave 'er side."

Gwendolyn had paid little attention to these conversations. Now something else the girl said filled her mind. "Mistress Sauda's brother, 'e is. Such a kind man. So eager to 'elp." Gwendolyn recalled the cream Sauda had made her wear.

"The rose can help." Gwendolyn took Jenna's hand, and they stood beneath the apple tree. "Conduct us to Paul's home," Gwendolyn commanded.

CHAPTER TWENTY

The castle garden was silent as a tomb as man and beast stared at one another. Paul shook with pain, but he knew the wound wasn't life-threatening. Of course, the man knew that too.

When Reinhardt spoke, his voice trembled. "I've always been grateful to your father. He was so kind. He could have refused to marry my sister after his father's death, but he chose to honor his father's wishes. He saved her as I could not. When we were children, Sauda would come to me, crying and bleeding from Father's attacks. I helped her as best I could. It was because of her that I chose to become a doctor. Father was a gambler, and when he lost money or drank his winnings away, Sauda and I were the recipients of his anger."

Reinhardt's face twisted with pain. "I threatened him one day, telling him I'd kill him if he ever hurt Sauda again, but he laughed at me. 'What will you do, weakling? Attack me with your flowers?'

"Perhaps I'm not strong. I never liked hunting like other boys, and I spent much time with plants. I used flowers and trees to make salves for Sauda's wounds. As she grew older, I made her cosmetics to enhance her beauty. Not that she wasn't lovely enough, but she constantly sought reassurance. Father belittled her constantly, and she needed my help." Reinhardt laughed, the laugh more a bitter cry than anything else.

"Precious little I could do for her! When Sauda died, my heart was torn in two. Justice demanded that Father pay for his treatment of her. Flowers can kill, and the ignorant fool should have realized that. It's quite simple to extract poison from willing plants, you know. They loved me as they loved Sauda. I placed poison into his nightly goblet of wine. I planned to take it to him, but I could not."

Reinhardt's face convulsed with pain. "He was right to call me a weakling. Every time I held that goblet in my hand, I saw Sauda's face. She was so pale when she was ill." He began to weep, his face flushing with anger. "Gustav loved Sauda—did you know that? He told me so. Everything was going so well. Then that witch had to interfere.

"After Sauda's death, I began my career as a physician. I'd failed my sister, but I determined to help others. I met Gustav often at the local tavern. I learned of your transformation from him. I feared for Gustav's life, and my fears were justified.

"One day, I found Gustav and his manservant lying dead in an apple orchard. The manservant was severely mauled. Gustav's wounds were not as severe, but he had obviously been attacked." He glared at Paul. "Can you imagine how I felt? I organized a search party, but we could never find you. The castle gates never yielded to us. Even battering rams were useless.

"I heard nothing about you for two years after that and assumed you were dead. Imagine my surprise when one of my friends entered these grounds. He's endured so much hardship, and now he's dying from despair. You killed one of his daughters. Your life is required for the ones you've taken."

Paul stared at Reinhardt, and in the man's eyes, he saw a reflection of himself. Loneliness and desperation were etched onto the man's visage.

"Father's and Claudio's deaths haunt me every day. I never meant to kill anyone. I would never kill Jenna. I let her go," Paul said.

"You expect me to believe that?" Reinhardt sneered. "You kill those who can't fight back and then hide. You're a coward." That same bitter laugh passed between his lips. "Mind you, I'm a coward as well, but I won't be today. You must be stopped!"

Paul rose, howling in fury. Despite his pain, he stood strong, towering above Reinhardt. "Leave here now," he growled.

Reinhardt shook his head. He raised his hand. Within it gleamed the butcher knife. He struck, sinking the knife into Paul's chest. Paul stumbled, his antlers connecting with Reinhardt's shoulder as he collapsed.

Man and beast fell in a crumpled heap.

CHAPTER TWENTY-ONE

Reinhardt lay in a welter of pain. The makeshift tourniquet he'd applied was inadequate, but it would suffice until he could bind his wound properly. His pain was irrelevant. Paul bled profusely. "Just a few moments more," Reinhardt whispered.

Paul wasn't listening to Reinhardt. He heard another voice, a voice of strength and compassion. *I'm here.*

Comfort caressed Paul's heart. A peculiar rustling surrounded him, and he saw a rose with rainbow hues open wider and wider. He gasped as a hand reached toward him. The hand hovered before Paul's face. *Touch me.*

Paul tried to lift a paw that he might caress the flower. Yet the pain was so great. "I cannot," he whispered.

Pierce me with your antlers.

Paul shuddered. He saw Claudio lying dead upon the ground. He shifted his gaze to Reinhardt. The man lay still. Addressing the rose, Paul whispered, "I'll kill you."

A poisoned rose transformed you. In order for the curse to be broken, I must die, as must you.

Paul trembled. He was dying now. Jenna was gone, and he was utterly alone. What did he have to lose? He raised his head and struck at the rose, his antlers sinking into the diaphanous petals.

A searing heat coursed through him, and Paul howled in agony. He watched as the rose crumpled before his eyes, the petals falling at an alarming rate. A hand stroked his head, laying him back upon the ground. The ground shook, and he heard the sound of a young woman whimpering with pain.

"Jenna?" he whispered. Then all was still.

CHAPTER TWENTY-TWO

J enna knelt within the castle gardens, clutching Paul's trembling body. She had arrived too late. She rocked to and fro, whimpering with pain. She caressed the antlers, the protruding eyes, and the marked cheek.

"Please don't leave me," she whispered. "I love you." She kissed his forehead and then drew back with a cry, feeling him go limp in her arms.

She heard someone stir beside her, and a familiar voice said, "He was telling the truth." Reinhardt patted Jenna's arm as he reached to take Paul from her.

"You killed him," Jenna whispered, her voice choked.

Reinhardt sighed wearily. "I did what I thought was best. I thought he'd killed you. How did you convince him to let you go?"

"You don't understand! He loves me, and I love him. He's kind."

Incredulity and fear filled Reinhardt's eyes. "Love him? Are you mad? He's bewitched you in some way, hasn't he?"

You're hurt, Reinhardt. A majestic voice, powerful even in its pain-racked intonation, filled the garden, and Reinhardt gasped, startled by the sound.

"Who's there?" he asked sharply.

I seek to heal your wounds.

Reinhardt's eyes alighted upon a mangled rose, its final petals preparing to fall. He thought he glimpsed a hand hovering just above the rose's petals, a hand that bore a strange wound. The hand was not clearly defined but seemed to cradle the rose's fragile head, and in the wound's center was a drop of blood that gleamed like a ruby. He felt a twinge of compassion. He was a Flower Master, after all.

Reinhardt thought of the many flowers and trees that he'd used in his fruitless quest to save Sauda's life. He'd made many medicines for her, spoon-feeding her his concoctions when she was too weak to lift her head. For a time, it had seemed as if his medicines were working, but that deformed witch's magic had been too strong. Anger slammed into his heart. He glared at the rose.

"I don't need healing, but others did, and no one helped them." He staggered to his feet, preparing to turn away.

It was then that he finally noticed another figure in the garden. The ugliest woman he'd ever seen knelt beside the dying rose. He recognized her immediately, and bile rose in his throat. "You," he hissed.

Gwendolyn gazed at Reinhardt, pain carved onto her face. "I'm sorry," she whispered.

"Are you? Now I suppose you want me to forgive you, and then we can go on our merry way. Sauda was so happy when Gustav married her. 'I love him,' she told me. 'I'll be a good wife to him.' She always suspected you were the one who sent that red rose on her wedding day. Now you have the gall to ask my forgiveness? You're more ignorant than I believed possible, witch."

He turned from her with contempt. It was then that he felt a weakness unlike anything he'd ever felt before. A heaviness pressed against his wounded shoulder.

"You're dying," Gwendolyn said. "Is that what you want? Accept the gift that Tecoptra offers you."

Reinhardt turned back to Gwendolyn. His hand was clenched around the handle of the bloodstained butcher knife he'd retrieved from the ground. He was shaking. His eyes strayed to the rose yet again. He saw that only one petal remained. It trembled and seemed so very fragile. Could one mere rose petal really save him? He thought of the apple tree he had wounded. The pain in his shoulder intensified. Reinhardt felt the knife growing heavier and heavier in his hand.

With an oath, he allowed his hand to relax, and the knife clattered to the ground. He bowed his head in defeat. He saw Sauda's wistful face on her wedding day. He saw Mirabel's kind visage. "I became a doctor because I had failed my sister," he whispered. "I'm a failure in all things. I'm so very tired."

He looked at Gwendolyn and then bowed his head. "Justice demands that you die," he said, "but I am too weak to carry it out." He gasped as another spasm of pain attacked him, and he crumpled to the ground.

The rose opened wider than ever, the final petal falling. A gentle breeze wafted the fragile petal toward Reinhardt's trembling hand.

Tecoptra is just, but he is also merciful. The pain-racked but powerful voice filled the garden once more.

Reinhardt felt someone gently touch his hand, moving it just close enough to the rose petal that the tips of his fingers grazed its bruised surface. Reinhardt managed to raise his head, and he saw that Gwendolyn's hand was holding his.

A strange heat tore through him, to be replaced by calming coolness. His eyes began to close. "I'm sorry," he whispered. "Miri, I truly loved you." Then he lay still.

Gwendolyn stared at Reinhardt's lifeless body and at the dead rose upon the ground.

She wept, turning to where Jenna knelt beside Paul. Rain began to fall, and the roses rustled, speaking one word: *Awaken.*

CHAPTER TWENTY-THREE

J enna continued caressing Paul's face. Suddenly, she felt something strange. His fur was gone. Was she mad? She felt him stir beneath her hand. She felt a broad forehead and soft tendrils of hair. She was definitely feeling skin, not animal fur. She gasped.

"Jenna," Paul whispered, his voice deep and familiar. "You came back."

Jenna flung her arms around Paul and helped him stand. Trailing her hands down his arms, her fingers encountered hands where paws had once been.

"I said I'd return," she said, laughing with joy.

Voices filled the gardens as a multitude of people joined them. The enchantment had broken, and the liberated servants laughed and embraced one another. Gwendolyn gazed at the happy celebration. As she observed the people, she also saw the rose, which now sparkled more vibrantly than ever. It had been restored.

She turned to Paul and Jenna, smiling as she watched them embrace. Behind her, the castle gate stood open, and she watched a man and young woman enter the garden. Gwendolyn knew they must be members of Jenna's family. The young woman ran to Reinhardt's side, reaching out to touch his hand. Her face grew pale.

Then Gwendolyn watched as Reinhardt sat up and stared around the garden. She saw his weary face break into a smile as his eyes focused on the young woman beside him.

"Miri," he whispered.

Gwendolyn breathed a prayer of thanksgiving and walked away, returning to her shop. She had a feeling that her services might be required in the future. In her mind, she saw a vibrant wedding bouquet of white roses.

Author's Note

The system for reading described in this story is historically accurate. Before the mid-nineteenth century, blind individuals read utilizing books with raised print letters. The system began in France in 1771 when Valentin Haüy, a civil servant, founded the Royal Institute for Blind Juveniles in Paris, France, the first school of its kind. To help students learn to read, he commissioned textbooks printed with raised letters. The system was impractical, for the books were cumbersome, and reading was slow. However, the system was the first step toward opening the door of reading and writing for blind individuals.

A blind student would later attend the institute that Haüy founded. The student was named Louis Braille. He developed his own system, which enabled individuals to read more efficiently.

In my own personal experience, I am indebted to Haüy and Braille, for God used them to demolish confining walls of ignorance. I look forward to meeting these men one day in order that I might thank them for their tremendous work.

To learn more about Valentin Haüy and Louis Braille, I recommend the excellent biography, *Triumph over Darkness: The Life of Louis Braille*, by Lennard Bickel.

CROSSING
TO
AFENDIA

DEDICATION

To my Heavenly Brother with inexpressible gratitude.
You are the Way across the infinite divide between
Life and Death.

And to Trent David Burton, the best earthly brother a sister
could have. Thank you for your support in all my adventures
and for the fun times we share.

Adopted girl from the Pacmana race will call forth the King's wondrous grace.

The Ancient Afendian Scrolls

Pointy-Ears! Pointy-Ears!" The ever-increasing multitude of girls danced round and round the huddled form, their jeers growing in volume. Several daring ones gathered stones, preparing to fling them into the young girl's face. "Your father and mother defied Hungali. You're no better than a donkey."

Faluri struggled to shift her weight, but the baskets strapped to her back prevented movement. She gritted her teeth and snarled in anger as she tried to free herself. Her skeletal frame buckled, and her back screamed in agony. She tried to plead for mercy, but fear and anger made her words emerge as unintelligible gibberish. A few of the girls backed away, their faces growing pale as they stared at her livid visage, the saliva streaming from her mouth, the teeth exposed in a vicious snarl.

A heavyset girl, her dazzling dress of cloth brocade glinting with jewels, retrieved a stick from the ground. Obviously the ringleader, she thrust the stick forward, jabbing Faluri's arm. "Get up and finish your task, donkey."

Faluri fought to stand, but the burden was simply too heavy. She had already fallen twice, and the girls had continued to strap baskets to her back. Curse her distended belly that constantly groaned with hunger! Curse the fruit seller who had momentarily left his stall! Curse the peach that had tasted of ambrosia!

How had she been expected to know that the basket of fruit had belonged to a nobleman's daughter? The glistening fruit had perched upon a shelf unattended, and the sweet scent had driven her mad. She had snatched the peach and started to flee but had been accosted by the heavyset girl, who had been perusing ribbons in a nearby stall.

"I-I didn't mean—"

"What's that? Bray louder." The girl laughed, preparing to use her stick for a second assault.

WHACK! A stone flew through the air, and Faluri cringed, fully expecting the missile to be meant for her. Instead, her tormentor screamed as her weapon sailed from her hands and fell into fragments.

A broad-shouldered young man emerged from where he had been concealed behind a tree. "Aren't you a bit old for such childishness, Ariadne?" he murmured. "Why don't you pick on someone who can fight back?"

Ariadne glared, her eyes glinting with malice. "Uncle Augustus will hear of this, Randolf," she hissed. "Father's already displeased with your disruptions of the counsel."

"And he'll do what, exactly? Send me to the cloisters? The Talmun monks are the only ones who speak the truth."

The girls gasped and turned away, quickly sinking to their knees and touching their foreheads to the earth. "Hungali will kill you one day," one of them said. "The cloisters under the monks' Talmun trees are accursed. You learn nothing but lies there."

"Their scrolls are the true ones," the man said.

Ariadne laughed. She flounced to Faluri's side, removing one of the baskets from her back and sauntering away. The other girls copied her movements. Faluri gasped as the burdens were removed, sighing in relief as her pounding heart subsided.

The man bent over her and smiled. He was probably no more than eighteen or nineteen, and his hazel eyes shone with kindness. He was not impressive looking, but rather plain. Yet something drew her to him, and she could not turn from his compassionate gaze.

The man extended his hand, offering to help her stand. Faluri shrank back, her eyes widening and another snarl escaping her lips.

"Do you bite?" The man grinned at her.

She could not help but smile, for he—had they called him Randolf?—drew back slightly.

"I won't touch you. I just thought you might need help."

Faluri struggled to her feet, her head spinning as she tried to get her bearings. She opened her mouth, but fear choked her words.

Randolf smiled at her. "You're welcome. Here." He drew a flask of water from the pocket of his tunic.

Faluri backed away yet again, her shoulders shaking. How often had she reached out only to receive slaps or worse?

Randolf shrugged. "You're so thin. Bet you're hungry. Come to my house. I'm sure Mother will help you."

Faluri turned to run away, but the boy's next words stopped her in her tracks. "We're having stuffed goose and apple meringues tonight. They're my favorite dishes."

Faluri turned toward him, her eyes growing wide. Apple meringues? Her mother used to make those. She fell

97

into step beside Randolf, never guessing that these first steps would set into motion such momentous events.

As she shuffled in his wake, she became aware of the pulsating ground. Was it her imagination, or was Hungali's heartbeat quickening? Moreover, did the quickening heartbeat signify anger or fear? She did not know, and she did not care.

She remembered the stories told around the hearth of her home. In the version of the story that everyone knew, there was a mountain kingdom that soared above their valley, the Kingdom of Afendia, the Land of Immortality and Perpetual Abundance. She had heard tell of a creature that had infiltrated the land, bringing poison in his wake. The creature had been as ugly as he was deadly, a creature who claimed to be king and demanded absolute allegiance. One of Afendia's most gifted inhabitants had resolved to save his land, but the king had forced him to leave. Many had followed him, descending the mountains to the valley below and establishing their own kingdom. Yet the creature often sought to take them away from their home, to force them back into his clutches.

Faluri thought of this story as she followed Randolf from the market. The canama fields lay just beyond a small hillock, the place that only held shame and misery. Randolf turned to the right, leading her up a winding pathway and away from the place of shame. Her mind continued to ponder the story that all the children knew, even the despised Pacmana race.

The alternate version of the story was startlingly different. Only a select few knew of it, for the story was sheer blasphemy. The Pacmana nation was the only race where certain individuals believed the sacrilegious tale. In that version, a benevolent king ruled the mountain land of

Afendia, providing for his subjects in every way. He stipulated that his subjects not leave the mountain, for the further a person descended, the thicker the air became. Darkness dwelled below the mountain peak, a lonely, depraved beast craving companionship. Darkness clawed at the ground with tenacious fingers, stuffing itself with emptiness and growing ever hungrier. It keened and wailed, pleading for someone to come. One man heard that cry and responded.

The man had attempted to usurp the king's throne. His attempt had failed, and in his anger, he had thrown himself from the mountain peak, darkness enveloping him. As he sank into the cold embrace, he felt his body collapse into a gaping chasm. Above him, he thought he glimpsed a hand reaching down as if to pull him up. He shrank from the proffered hand, dwindling into the chasm's depths. He was no longer a servant of darkness but darkness itself. His name was Hungali. He keened and thrashed in agony, calling for others to come to him. Many had done so until the land beneath the mountain had become its own settlement.

Faluri had never believed the latter version of the story, but her mother had done so. "My child, if you look into the night sky, you'll see a shimmering white star shaped like a hand. The hand is Elumi's, my child: the Great King who seeks to help us, to bring us home."

Faluri had strained her eyes, seeking the hand that her mother constantly claimed to see. Yet the fog that enveloped their land prevented her from seeing anything.

"Home, Mother? But this is our home. We have all we need."

Her mother had frowned and gently tousled her daughter's carrot-colored hair. "Do we deserve to be treated as animals? The true scrolls say that in Afendia, there is no slavery. One day, child, I will take you with me, and we will cross to Afendia. We will be reunited with your father. His illness robbed us of many years, but he will see you one day, and we will live together again."

Yet that day had never come, for her mother had become very ill, with an illness that seemed to come from nowhere. Great spasms coursed through her body, and she burned with fever. She grew increasingly thin until she was little more than a skeleton, her usually rosy cheeks wan. She had called Faluri to her side two weeks after the illness struck.

Speaking through parched lips, she said, "He reaches for me, and I will go to him. He reaches for you too. He is even now in this land, and he will care for you. I will always be with you." Then, she lay back on her pillows, her eyes closing in sleep.

The next morning, she was gone. No trace of her remained, but a scent lingered behind, a scent of cinnamon, cloves, and other spices.

"Are you all right?"

Randolf's soft inquiry jarred Faluri from her reverie. She nodded.

"You can speak to me if you want to." He grinned at her.

Faluri swallowed. "I-I snuck away from the canama fields last night. I-I was hungry. I didn't mean to steal anything. The overseers will—"

"You'll be fine at my home. Mother will want to fatten you up. It'll be all right."

Faluri shuddered, her eyes filling with tears. "Why did you help me?"

"Because you needed it. Besides, my cousin is spoiled. She needed to be put in her place. Uncle Locmana won't do anything, so—"

"B-but I am a Pacmana maiden. They did what was expected."

"By whom?"

Faluri blinked in confusion. "Why, by everyone, of course."

"Not by me." Randolf grinned at her and turned onto a stone pathway.

Faluri gasped as she beheld a towering mansion, a dwelling made entirely of glittering stone. Ivory gates stood at the dwelling's entrance.

"Randolf! Randolf!" A petite girl pelted through the gates as her brother prepared to open them. Her dimpled cheeks were flushed, and she jumped up and down with excitement. "Poppa got me a pony today. Will you teach me to ride?"

Randolf scooped up the child in his arms, swinging her round and round until she squealed in delight. Depositing her on the ground, he darted across the courtyard, beginning a spontaneous game of tag. The girl chased him, her shrill laughter filling the air. After a few moments, she collapsed in an exhausted heap, giggling and grinning. Randolf plopped down beside her.

"Yes, I'll teach you," he panted, tousling the girl's hair. "Now, Naolia, meet the young lady I brought home."

Naolia gaped, quickly standing and turning to Faluri. "You're a Pacmana maiden. You have pointed ears. The stories are true."

Randolf frowned at his sister. "She has beautiful eyes, Naolia, and her ears are unique."

Faluri flushed. No one had ever told her that her eyes were beautiful. And surely what he said was absurd. Pointy ears were a disgrace.

Naolia's face fell as she held out her hand. "I'm sorry," she murmured.

In spite of herself, Faluri smiled. "It's all right." Tentatively, she clasped the little girl's hand in hers.

"Come on," Randolf said. "We all better go inside."

"You are impossible, Randolf!"

Faluri jerked awake, her full belly groaning with discomfort and her heart pounding. She recognized the voice of Randolf's father, a burly man with an impassive face.

"We can't keep her here. Have you any idea the wrath that will descend upon us?"

"Augustus, please." The soft murmurings of Randolf's mother filled the silence. "You'll awaken the girl."

"The rules are binding, Melinda. He'll bring trouble upon us by his constant defiance of the counsel."

"What rules, Father?" Randolf's voice was as soft as ever, but a hint of steel permeated it.

"The counsel's, of course. The class distinction is unbreachable. I'm sorry about it, but I cannot defy it."

"Why not?"

"Because I . . ." Augustus' voice trailed away.

"Remember the Afendian scrolls, Father? 'Adopted girl from the Pacmana race will call forth the King's wondrous grace.' "

"B-but we cannot be the ones to—"

"Oh come now, Augustus," Melinda murmured. "How can you, of all people, say that? What kind of people would we be if we turned her out? She obviously has no one."

Faluri listened to this exchange in utter confusion, her eyes filling with tears. What was to become of her?

The next morning, she learned the answer. Tentatively rising from the luxurious canopied bed upon which she'd slept, she made her way to the large dining room. Randolf held out his hand, guiding her to the table upon which sat a lavish breakfast.

"Welcome home," he said.

"You're a fool, Augustus!" The raspy voice reverberated in the grand hallway, charged with an overpowering anger. "To even have one of them in your home means trouble. Moreover, to express your intention of adopting—"

"She has no one, Locmana. Randolf brought her here a fortnight ago, the most emaciated child I'd ever seen. How could I turn her away? Melinda feels the same."

"You'll rain down Hungali's anger upon us! You know the prophecy as well as anyone. The Pacmana race will bring down the foul creature from the mountains of Afendia, and he will devour us all."

"I know what the new scrolls say, but the ancient ones extol the Pacmana race as equal to our own."

"You dare to reference those blasphemous writings? What has come over you? My own brother listening to the rantings of a foolish young upstart! Randolf has no proof that those writings are genuine. Ever since he returned from his studies, he's been an outspoken fool. He does not know what he's saying."

"You speak of my son and your own nephew! You may be lord of this land, but you're also my brother, Locmana. If you cannot respect your own family's decisions, then I'll thank you to leave this house!"

"That animal will ruin you all—you see if she doesn't!"

Locmana's footsteps slammed down the hall as he stormed from the house. Faluri stood stock-still in the shadows, her mind reeling and her heart pounding. She turned and hurried to the rear entrance of the mansion, her eyes brimming with tears. Was the noble family that had done so much for her truly in danger? What of Randolf, who had been nothing but kind?

Faluri hurried through a patch of blackberry bushes, journeying to the road that would take her to the marketplace.

"Oh, it's the Pacmana donkey!" A familiar, jeering voice emerged from beyond the blackberry hedge. Faluri cringed and tried to retreat, but Ariadne flounced into view. Her face was flushed with triumph.

"What are you doing out here alone? Is Randolf not holding your hand anymore?"

"Leave me alone." Faluri's voice emerged in a pathetic squeak. Her mind was jerked back to the humiliating day in the marketplace.

"No. I think you still owe me for that peach you stole. Besides, you don't belong here." For the first time, Ariadne's sneer faltered, a look of fear crossing her face. "My father told me. You'll ruin everything."

Faluri blinked. "Ruin what? I'm doing nothing wrong."

"Idiot! Your being born was wrong. You'll bring that creature from the mountains down upon us. He'll kill us all."

"I don't under—"

My pretty one. Come to me.

A gentle voice suddenly burst upon the girls' ears. The ground began to pulsate more strongly than ever, a heartbeat of ecstatic anticipation.

A gentle breeze began to blow, carrying with it a strangely cloying scent unlike anything either girl had smelled before. The blackberry bushes bent beneath the wind's assault, parting as if to let someone pass.

You're so lovely. Come and be mine.

As the breeze advanced, it grew stronger and stronger. Ariadne gaped and then turned and ran, her face ashen.

The strange presence seemed to pause for a moment, a deep-throated laugh emanating from it. *The weaklings always run, but you shall not.*

Faluri struggled against the breeze, which was no longer gentle. The ground began to quake. Shaking, she fell to her knees, pressing her forehead to the ground in supplication. "G-great Hungali. Please—"

Yes, my dear? The breeze surrounded her now, pummeling her from all sides. Gentle hands picked her up, clutching her in a grip that was suddenly as strong as iron. *I am here with you. I am taking you to my home, for my loneliness grows daily.*

Faluri whimpered, and she suddenly realized that her mother had spoken the truth. She tried to scream, to make even the smallest outcry, but Hungali's hold prevented speech. She felt the breeze move at a lightning pace, traversing miles in seconds. She was being carried she knew not where.

Faluri's head swam in confusion. As her eyes adjusted to her surroundings, she realized that she stood upon a walkway of stone. Two jutting walls were on either side of her, and her head spun as she realized she stood at a dizzying height. Coldness bit into her. She saw two snow-capped mountain peaks beyond the walls, their white faces staring impassively at her predicament. More mountains watched from across the chasm. The breeze had lessened in intensity.

Welcome, sweet one. Hungali's voice emerged from her right, but Faluri could see no one. She dared to turn her head and immediately regretted her mistake.

A chasm loomed at the edge of the walkway, so vast as to be unbelievable. The sheer drop yawned up at her like a gaping mouth. Pinpricks of light danced before Faluri's eyes as she strained to catch a glimpse of the bottom, but it was clear that this chasm was bottomless. The ground itself moved here, seeming to breathe of its own accord. Faluri's knees buckled as her heart plummeted in fear.

It's frightening, I know. Hungali's tones were caressing, his voice dripping with a musical cadence as sweet as syrup. *I was frightened as well. Yet I cast myself from his land of obligation and ingratitude. I embraced my own destiny.*

Faluri trembled, her mouth growing dry. "Y-you are no longer who you were, no longer a brilliant man."

Precisely, clever girl. I am a god. Yet godhood is rather trying at times. The loneliness is overwhelming.

"My father and mother. You killed them, didn't you?" Tears sprang to her eyes, but she tried to hold them back. She did not want this creature to see her weep.

Why do you mortals always cry? It is demeaning and accomplishes nothing. Contempt laced his voice. Then, he resumed his gentle tones. *Killing is such a harsh term. I did nothing. It was their fault. They refused to listen to my warning. I told them to give you to me, yet they refused to do so.*

Faluri thought of her mother's final days of illness. "You're a monster."

The air from the chasm swelled in a roaring torrent, and the ground quaked violently. Faluri trembled, quickly stammering, "I-I am sorry. What do you want from me?"

I told you! I want you for my own. All you need do is come to me. Just cast yourself into my embrace.

Faluri stepped backward, her eyes growing round with horror. "Never!"

Then I shall wreak havoc on the land. My wrath will know no bounds, for I will make the Pacmana nation and the nobles suffer beyond anything they have ever dreamed.

"Faluri!" A voice, an honest, human voice, burst upon her. It came from her left. Faluri sighed in relief. She knew that voice. Turning, she saw Randolf's strong arm beckoning to her from behind the jutting stone wall. "Grab onto me."

Faluri stared at her surroundings. His hand was far enough away that she dared not reach toward it. One false step, and she would hurtle into Hungali's arms.

As if to confirm her suspicion, the ground quaked yet again, a derisive laugh filling the air. *You fool! You think a mere mortal's handclasp will save you?*

"What are you frightened of, Hungali? That the prophecies are true? 'Adopted girl from the Pacmana race will call forth the King's wondrous grace.' " Randolf's voice soared above the laughter.

I destroyed those prophecies long ago.

"The prophecies will never die." Randolf continued to proffer his hand. He addressed Faluri. "Ariadne found me. She said you'd been taken. I was desperate to find you, and a breeze picked me up. I found myself here. Please let me help you. I was so angry that day the bullies were tormenting you. I thought of how I would have reacted if

Naolia had been in that situation. You're a sister to me, just as she is."

Faluri knew that a decision had to be made. Trembling, she turned from the chasm, reaching out her hand toward Randolf.

Instantly, the chasm roiled, a clattering sound as of pounding hoofbeats emerging from its depths. Faluri dared one look back and saw a coal-black steed. Fire spewed from the steed's mouth as it thundered from the chasm and onto the walkway. The animal was not solid, but was formed out of darkness itself. The air that comprised Hungali's being had transformed into this massive beast. It charged at Faluri, stones from the walkway hurtling into the void below.

Faluri closed her eyes, desperately groping for Randolf's hand. Warm fingers closed over her own, and she was lifted into the air with a tremendous jerk and deposited onto a snow-covered hill. A tremendous shattering sound assaulted her ears, and she opened her eyes in time to see the walkway begin to break apart.

The horse stood in midair and lunged at Randolf, who stood directly in front of Faluri, shielding her from the oncoming attack. Faluri saw the steed's massive body collide with Randolf. Transforming back into the swirling air, Hungali shoved Randolf toward the gaping chasm.

Faluri screamed as her brother plummeted into the chasm. The air that comprised Hungali's being pressed down hard, suffocating him. She saw the walkway shake violently, and stones broke away from its surface, hurtling into the chasm's depths. The stones struck Randolf again and again as they fell.

"No! No!"

As she screamed, Hungali's crazed laughter and the thundering tattoo of his heartbeat pounded out a drunken swell of triumph.

Faluri lunged toward the shaking walkway, desperate to somehow rescue Randolf, but something pushed her back, a breeze that smelled of cinnamon, cloves and other strange spices. She felt herself being lifted, and blackness engulfed her. As she sank into sleep, she heard Hungali's angry vow: *You'll return to me even if I have to kill everyone else, pretty one. I'll make them give you up!*

Two Months Later

Faluri heard the groans and cries before she reached the fields. The clash of whips brought bile to her throat. She had worked in these fields so often with her mother. Now, she paused before the vast stretch of swaying canama plants. Women struggled under heavy baskets, which were strapped to their backs. They crawled along the ground, gathering stalks of canama. Young girls stood in a colossal pit, their hands and feet moving in a rhythmic dance as they used mallets to crush canama stalks into coarse granules of sugar. Men struggled to unload heavy crates of the freshly prepared sugar into colossal chests.

Above this activity loomed five burly men, each of them wearing crimson robes. They held whips in their hands as they marched through the fields. Faluri gasped as a young girl paused in the rhythm of the dance, slumping forward and crying with exertion. The mallet fell from her trembling hand, and she bent to retrieve it.

SWISH! SWISH! One of the overseers paused beside the pit, his whip crashing upon the little girl's shoulders.

Faluri bolted toward the pit. She lunged at the overseer, attempting to snatch the whip.

"Stay back, beast!" The overseer shoved Faluri backward, delivering a vicious blow to her stomach. She gasped and struggled to reach the pit, to cradle the young girl and bring her comfort.

"Wait." One of the other overseers approached at the sound of the commotion. He scrutinized Faluri closely, grabbing one of her hands. "Soft as goat cheese," he murmured. "You don't belong here, despite your obvious Pacmana status. A house slave, eh?" He leered at her. "What brings you here?"

Faluri shuddered, longing to back away from his scrutiny. Yet she also realized that he had given her a golden opportunity, and she must make the most of it. "Lord Locmana sent me here to retrieve another girl for the kitchens."

The overseer frowned. "Do you take me for a fool? His Lordship has been ill for a week. He can't even rise from his bed. Why are you really here?"

"I'm telling you the truth. Some dignitaries are coming for a banquet tomorrow, and we're short-staffed."

The overseer leant closer to her, his leer more pronounced than ever. "Wench thinks she can pull one over on me, does she?" he chortled. "I'll just put you to work till I can verify your story."

Faluri stared. "Y-you'll pay for your mistreatment of me."

The overseer laughed. "Lord Locmana couldn't care less what happens to you swine." He shoved her toward the pit.

As she fell into the gaping hole, the deep thrumming of the earth immediately pulled at her, forcing her to rise and move in tandem with its rhythm. She struggled with all her might to resist, but the pulsating heartbeat brutally pummeled her.

"You must obey him," a little girl whispered. "If you don't, you'll be beaten."

Faluri gasped and turned to the familiar voice. With a strangled cry, she reached out a hand to the petite, auburn-haired girl, the only one whose ears were not pointed. "Naolia," she whispered. "It's me."

"The herald read the proclamation to us," Naolia whispered. Both girls were continuing to crush the stalks, a task that should have been relatively easy. Yet the mallets were so heavy, and the pulsating ground made the girl's legs throb with fatigue. "We have to be in the market square at noon tomorrow."

"I know. I came to tell you that you have to escape."

"But I can't. Father and Mother—"

"You must! Don't you understand? I am the reason you're here in the fields. I'm the reason Randolf is gone."

Faluri shuddered as another spasm of memories struck her, and she sank into their insistent clutches.

The breeze had deposited her at the servants' entrance of Lord Locmana's grand mansion. She had been found by a scullery maid and had been appointed as a serving maid herself. She refused to tell anyone where she was from.

The plague had begun the next day, and twenty noblemen had died. Then, Lord Locmana had been stricken with the mysterious illness himself, and hysteria had grown to a fever pitch. The lord had decreed that a Pacmana maiden must be sacrificed to appease Hungali's wrath and had said that the casting of lots would determine the maiden to be chosen.

Now, as Faluri relived these memories, it suddenly came to her that the casting of lots was merely a clever ruse. She had always been the object of Hungali's desire, and he was determined to have her. She thought of Randolf. He had sacrificed himself so that she might live. Should she not do the same for his sister?

Hungali had been as good as his word, for the unexplained illnesses of so many noble young men had caused outright panic. Blame had naturally fallen on the Pacmana race. Only Faluri's adopted family had taken a stand, for though they did not know where Faluri was, they extolled the Pacmana race as equals to the nobles. Thus, they were punished by being forced to become slaves.

Faluri stared at her adopted sister for a long moment. Then, she whispered to herself, "He knew I'd give myself up to protect you, to honor Randolf's memory." There was no need to wait for the drawing of lots. She would do what she had to do tonight.

"Sweeties. Lovely sweeties!" An old man's voice rang through the relentless pounding of the mallets and groans of the slaves. Faluri stared as she beheld a stooped form hobbling through the crowd of slaves. The overseers flocked to the man, snatching sweets from a basket that he balanced upon his hip.

"Easy!" he cried. "Plenty for all!"

"All? These beasts don't get anything." One of the overseers guffawed, his mouth so crammed with canama sugar that his words were garbled. Syrup dribbled down his chin.

"Beasts, eh?" The man chortled, grinning cheekily. "Appears to be only you yourself. Beast in the decidedly singular. Where's my coin? These treats aren't free, you know."

"Watch your tongue, you old fool! We've never paid in the past, have we?" The overseer yanked the basket from the old man's hand, dividing the remaining goodies among himself and the others. "Be off with you."

Calmly, the man raised his hands, snatching the basket back. The wicker container now bulged with a vast profusion of treats, and he staggered under its weight. The overseers gaped at his retreating form as he circulated among the slaves, giving each one a cone of canama sugar. "From King Elumi's own fields. Not ill-gotten by slave labor but freely grown for all."

As the man made his rounds, he stopped beside the pit, gently patting each girl on the shoulder as he handed them the treats. "Only one day more," he murmured. "Then your slavery will cease."

As he spoke these words, his eyes locked onto Faluri, who gasped in shock. "You are more than you think, courageous girl," the sweet-seller murmured. "Hungali wanted you to surrender to his embrace. Now, he will surrender to you."

He withdrew a cloth bag and a belt the translucent color of honey from the folds of his brown tunic. Thrusting these items into Faluri's hands, he enfolded her in a strong embrace. His touch brought a surge of comfort and strength, and the scents of cinnamon, cloves, and other spices clung to him. Faluri suddenly knew from whence the breeze that had carried her to the mansion had originated. Then the man vanished.

Faluri blinked in wonder at the bag. Trembling, she opened it and stared in disappointment. A lump of canama sugar, a skein of scarlet yarn, and a strangely scented leaf were the only objects it contained. Faluri withdrew the leaf, gaping at its strange beauty. The leaf was scallop-edged and shone with a mesmerizing brilliance. Faluri returned the leaf to the bag, her mind reeling with confusion. She prepared to journey to her doom.

The canama fields were eerily silent after night fell. Faluri stood alone, her hands trembling. Around her waist was the golden belt, and attached to it was the small cloth bag. She felt the thrumming of Hungali's heartbeat and knew what she had to do. Stepping to the edge of the canama pit, she prepared to enter it yet again.

A thunderous pounding of hoofbeats tore through the silence, and Faluri shrank back, fully expecting the ghostly black steed to rise from the pit's depths. Yet the sound came from behind her.

Trembling, she turned around and came face-to-face with a towering steed. The horse's coat was dazzlingly white, and a scarlet mane flowed down its neck. The horse neighed and reared onto its hind legs, and she realized that it was wild. Yet even in its wildness, it stood before her, its glittering golden eyes scrutinizing her closely.

Faluri reached into the bag at her waist and withdrew the lump of canama sugar, a sugar more refined than any grown in these fields. She proffered the sweet, and the horse bent forward, its mouth nuzzling her fingers as it took it from her hand. The majestic animal nickered softly and knelt upon the ground. Light poured from its shimmering mane, and Faluri caught the distinct scent of cinnamon, cloves, and other strange spices.

"Y-you will allow me to ride upon your back?" Her heart pounded in fear, but her eyes were filled with tears of wonder. "I must journey to the mountains."

The horse inclined its head. Faluri grasped its mane and clambered upon its back. Instantly, the horse rose and began to gallop, its hooves thundering across the fields. The steed's movements were so graceful, and Faluri's hair flew behind her in a gentle breeze. The horse's movements grew even faster, and they were suddenly airborne. Faluri gasped, clinging to the mane with an iron grip.

Soon, Faluri felt familiar biting cold, and she felt a tremendous jolt as the horse landed upon a stone walkway. To her right yawned the immense chasm, and everything was as she remembered from that harrowing day. The only difference was that now there was no one to lend her a helping hand. Even as she thought this, the steed vanished, and the ground began to quake.

Ah! I knew you would return. Hungali's rumbling voice rang with jubilant triumph. *Your weak heart could not bear that others die. You're so pathetic!*

Faluri swallowed, staring as the breeze began to intensify. "Y-you want me to come to you. Why? You love no one but yourself."

Have you any inkling of how hard I've worked to establish my kingdom? The prophecy will not be fulfilled. Once I have dealt with you, then I will be safe. My reign will be firmly established. That interfering mortal sought to save you, and I dealt with him. No one can liberate you from my hands.

Faluri felt the tears course down her cheeks, and she thought of Randolf's intervention. "My brother is strong, far stronger than you'll ever be."

There was a long silence. Then, Hungali spoke again. *What do you wear around your waist?* His voice was strangely different, the voice of a curious child.

Faluri trembled, clutching the bag in her sweat-soaked hand.

Come now. Let me see.

Faluri held the bag toward the gaping chasm, keeping the contents hidden from sight. "I'll show you if you'll consent to remove the illness from the land."

Hungali laughed. *You presume to bargain with me?*

"This bag contains great weapons from King Elumi's own land. Would you not desire to possess them yourself?"

The air from the chasm roared in anger, jerking Faluri's tunic as it pummeled her extended hand. *Give it to me!*

"I must have your word first."

Very well, shrewd creature. I will remove the plague, but you will not leave here alive. I'll have you and the weapons as well. Now give me the bag.

Faluri opened her hand, reaching toward the roiling breeze. Instantly, iron fingers snatched the bag away, tearing it open to expose the contents.

A snarl of utter rage erupted in the air. *You deceived me! What is the meaning of this?*

The bag was flung into the air in disgust. It flew toward Faluri's outstretched hand. Hungali's aim was wrong, for the bag clattered onto the stone walkway at Faluri's feet, the white leaf and the scarlet skein of yarn erupting from their cloth enclosure.

Suddenly, the overpowering scent that Faluri knew so well filled the air. She gasped as a Talmun tree appeared where the leaf had fallen, a squat object from which dazzling light poured forth. The tree's golden branches swayed, and its dazzlingly white leaves glimmered.

Hungali's laughter was horrible to hear. *You think a mere tree will stop me?*

Another massive tree, this one the size of a great oak, burst from the chasm's depths, its towering branches a garish black. The tree bent forward, the snake-like branches wrapping themselves around the smaller Talmun tree. The small trunk snapped, the deafening pop resembling the sound of a breaking back, and the Talmun tree hurtled into the chasm's depths.

Your games bore me.

As these words rumbled around her, Faluri's attention was arrested by the glimmering scarlet yarn that still lay on the stone walkway. The skein was unraveling by itself, the glimmering thread stretching until it reached the lip of the chasm. The yarn continued to unwind, stretching until a thin rivulet of scarlet spanned the infinite divide. Faluri realized she was staring at a bridge.

I see. Yet another tiresome tactic. Hungali rose upward, suddenly transforming into the handsomest man Faluri had ever seen. His jet-black hair billowed around him like a cape, and his fathomless eyes shone with triumph. Calmly, he reached out a hand, clutching the thin rope bridge. In an almost human voice, he said, "I will break this as I destroyed that useless tree."

Hungali's boasts were futile, for the harder he pulled at the scarlet thread, the weaker he seemed to become. Faluri saw him shake with exertion.

"Hungali." A voice shattered the stillness, and the scarlet thread seemed to move. Faluri saw a form in the distance, a man walking toward her with measured strides. "Your day of reckoning has come."

That voice! That compassionate, powerful voice! Faluri gasped in shock as she beheld Randolf's approaching form. He walked upon the glimmering bridge, his scarred hands held out in front of him. His face shone with a translucent light.

Hungali lunged toward Randolf, his face contorted with rage. The man's form dwindled before Faluri's eyes, and the powerful breeze pushed against Randolf's advancing figure, repeatedly attempting to hurl him yet again into the cavernous depths.

It is not possible! You were crushed.

"Faluri, come to me." Randolf continued crossing the bridge, heedless of Hungali's rants.

Yes, Faluri. Go to him. Step upon this futile bridge. It will not bear a mortal's weight. When you fall, I shall be waiting to catch you. You shall melt into my embrace, and we shall become one. Hungali's jeers pummeled Faluri's stomach, and her heart quaked with fear.

"I will enable you to cross, Faluri. Do not be afraid. King Ellumi raised me back to life. I died for you, my sister, and a life freely given will bring death to ruin. I asked King Elumi to help me rescue our land, and he chose you to be the first to cross the chasm to his domain. Did King Elumi not give you sustenance in the canama fields? Did he not transport you here? Did not his branches weaken Hungali's power?"

Faluri stared, seeing within Randolf all the things that he was: a loving brother, a devoted friend, and a bridge builder. Shaking, she took her first tentative step toward the gaping chasm. In her ears, she heard Hungali's laughter. When she stepped onto the bridge, she felt it sway and give. The breeze grew so furious that she heard as if in a recurring nightmare the walkway begin to collapse yet again. The bridge groaned as it swayed to and fro. A scream erupted from her throat.

"The bridge will not collapse, Faluri. Trust me."

Her heart in her mouth, Faluri took another step forward, her right hand extended. Warm fingers closed over her own, and she and Randolf began to walk forward together. The bridge continued to sway and shake violently, but Faluri clung to her brother's strong hand.

As they reached the other side, they stepped from the bridge onto a snowcapped mountain peak. Instantly, the bridge ceased shaking, and in the distance, Faluri saw a towering Talmun tree burst from the chasm's depths. She saw now why the Talmun monks reverenced the trees.

As the tree emerged, Hungali was thrown back into the chasm. A low rumble emerged from the chasm's depths as the ground closed with a thunderous roar. The chasm had closed forever. Hungali's screams were abruptly silenced.

Faluri flung herself into Randolf's embrace. Brother and sister twirled round and round, and Faluri saw a dazzling sight. Vast canama fields stretched before her, the pure snow blanketing them in a profusion of downy white. The air was crisp and caressing, and the scents of cinnamon, cloves, and other unidentifiable spices tickled her nostrils.

This beauty was unsurpassed, but as Faluri stared, she glimpsed a sight more wondrous than any landscape. People worked in the fields side by side. No overseers plied their whips. People of every color and class were united here. In the distance, she saw two figures, a petite woman and a muscular man. Both of them sported pointed ears, and their faces were a mirror image of her own.

Suddenly, Faluri was running, her pace as swift as a mountain gazelle's. As she ran, the two figures ran as well, their eyes shining. Daughter, father, and mother met in a blinding collision, their tears of joy mingling together as they embraced.

Then King Elumi was there, enfolding the family into his arms and gently wiping the tears from their eyes. Faluri saw within his kind visage a shadow of the sweet-sellers smile. But it was merely a shadow of all of the things King Elumi was.

"Welcome to Afendia," he said, his voice like the rushing of many waters. "Welcome home."

Two days later, a brother and sister descended a vast mountain. They trod upon a walkway of scarlet stone, which was skirted by two Talmun trees. The trees stood like strong, silent sentries.

The brother and sister journeyed to a valley in search of willing pilgrims, travelers who would accompany them to a new home, a land of perpetual joy. The Chasm Crossers would make many journeys of this kind, and all would be well. The prophecy had been fulfilled. An adopted girl from the Pacmana race had called forth the King's wondrous grace.

DEDICATION

With inexpressible thanksgiving to my Savior, Jesus Christ,
who enables me to journey
through this often-treacherous world and who provides
safe passage to uncharted lands.

In memory of Stella Readus, a courageous, funny, and life-
loving warrior. She is a friend whom I deeply miss,
but I know she is experiencing adventures that are
unforgettable.

CHAPTER ONE

*Y*ou must listen carefully, my princess."

Bianca stared into the earnest blue eyes of the man she so rarely saw. Father was often away from the plantation, and his visits to her were welcome. He smiled upon her tenderly. "Will you listen for me once again?"

Bianca swallowed nervously. "Sometimes, I cannot hear the singing, Father," she said softly.

Simon Reginald nodded. He was willing to wait. The girl was always anxious to help, and she rarely disappointed him. He perused his daughter's innocent face: the skin of pristine snow, the ebony hair, and the ruby-red lips. Bianca was twelve now. How quickly time marched along! He smiled at his daughter.

"There is no hurry," he said. "Let this just be a day for us to spend together. I brought your favorite." He gestured to a picnic basket.

Bianca's eyes widened at the sight of such a large basket. "Ham and cheese sandwiches?" she asked.

Father grinned. "Naturally. And potato pancakes with apple butter."

Bianca's stomach rumbled with hunger. She leaned back on the cushioned seat of the carriage and relaxed. Father and daughter rode along in companionable silence.

Finally, Bianca asked, "How is Edward? Is he any better?"

"His illness vanishes for a time and then returns. Gloria is beside herself with worry."

Bianca nodded. Like her stepmother, she too worried constantly. Images of Stepbrother filled Bianca's mind, his wan face and pleading eyes. She often brought him treats from the kitchen. Once she had brought him a bouquet of wildflowers to brighten his nursery. He had smiled at her.

"I want to go outside like you," he had said hopefully. "Will you take me?"

Bianca had nodded. She would have taken him immediately, but the physicians were quite adamant that he needed to stay confined. The name of Edward's illness was unknown, and they feared that his sickness could worsen at the least provocation.

"I'll take you outside someday soon," she said emphatically. "I promise." She had hugged him tightly, feeling his frail body and fevered skin.

Bianca hung her head. What good was her promise if she couldn't even give Edward what he needed most? "I have tried, Father. I promise I have." Guilt slunk from its den, patting Bianca's shoulder in reprimand. She swallowed. "I will listen harder."

"That is all I ask," Father said gently. "That you try." He motioned for the driver to stop the carriage.

Simon reached for Bianca's hand and helped her down from the conveyance. "Isaac, look after the horses," he instructed, gesturing to the driver. The man nodded stiffly, his black-velvet skin shining with sweat.

Simon turned to Bianca. "Come. We'll eat first. You need strength for what's ahead."

Bianca surveyed the meadow in which they stood. Spring wore her garments in abundant array. Veriana was lovely in springtime. Bianca relished the rare occasions when she was allowed to leave the plantation.

She watched as Father spread a blanket on the ground and arranged their picnic. In addition to the sandwiches, there were dressed eggs and a jar of pickles. Bianca's attention was arrested by a small jar that she knew contained apple butter. She had helped the slaves to make the spread.

Father did not know that, of course. He would have been very angry, as she was forbidden to socialize with them.

But the days were long, and time always stretched before her like an unraveling skein of yarn. Bianca remembered how Priscilla had told her to go back inside. But the work had been fun! Her arms had moved rhythmically as she stirred the boiling apple and sugar mixture again and again until it was the perfect consistency. The work had been tiring, and she had sweated profusely, but the sense of accomplishment had been worth the fatigue. Apple butter was her favorite preserve, perhaps because she knew it was Father's favorite as well.

Bianca began to eat. She drank a concoction called dandy fizz, a drink that fairly danced in her cup and laughed as it slid silkily down her throat. "Thank you for summoning me today, Father," she said.

Father smiled. "I know how you enjoy our times together," he said.

Bianca nodded earnestly. "I miss you when you are—"

PLINK! PLINK! CHING! CHING! CHING!

Bianca's hands grew limp as her stomach plummeted. No! Not this soon! Her day with Father had barely begun!

The music swelled around her, a cacophonous refrain. The treasure was alive, and it called to her with supplication. *Come. We are here!* Bianca shuddered as the entreaty took hold of her in waves.

She had first heard the earth speak when she was nine. The gift of hearing the earth was uncommon, and Bianca knew of no one else who possessed it. Lately, the gift had seemed more like a curse.

Simon was instantly alert. Bianca's face had grown even whiter, and sweat covered her brow. "Child," he said urgently, grabbing the girl's arm. "You hear it, don't you? Where is it?"

Bianca was silent, and Simon shook her arm impatiently. "I must know! Tell me!"

With trembling hands, Bianca pointed to her left. "The Hart's Tears lie to the west," she whispered.

Father smiled and enfolded the trembling girl into his arms. "Well done," he said.

Bianca managed to nod in weak gratitude for the praise before she fell into unconsciousness.

Chapter Two

G loria Reginald knelt beside the canopied bed. Her bejeweled fingers caressed her young son's forehead. *He burns,* she thought wildly.

Edward was three summers old, and he was never well. Occasionally, the fever would abate, for Simon procured many medicines. But the illness would always return.

Gloria lowered her head to the mattress, allowing her tears to flow. Edward's birth had been so complicated, the labor so strenuous that the physicians had said Gloria could bear no more children. Edward was her only joy and her only offering to her husband.

Gloria rose to her feet. She ran a hand through her chestnut hair, making certain the ornamented combs were still in their appropriate places. She would not appear bedraggled and homely. Appearances mattered. She approached her vanity table and retrieved the heart-shaped mirror that sat atop it. She gazed upon herself, the crimson frock with the multitudes of ribbons threaded through the bodice, the glinting bejeweled combs that caused her to shine. She sighed with relief. Cosmetics would conceal the lines of fatigue etched onto her face. Perhaps Simon would—

"Mistress!"

The chamber door burst open, and Gloria turned, gasping as the slave woman entered. The woman's ebony skin was streaked with perspiration, and she was shaking. Her scarred left cheek stood out garishly. "I apologize for disturbing you, Mistress. It is Bianca. She is ill."

Gloria placed her mirror on the vanity and bestowed upon the slave a look of weary indifference. "What is the meaning of this disturbance?" she asked impassively.

She only hoped her voice would not betray the surge of molten anger that coursed through her veins. The nerve of him! After she had pleaded with Simon not to summon—

She lowered her gaze from the slave woman's earnest eyes so that she might regain her composure. Finally, she said, "You have no right to be here. The child is my responsibility, not yours."

"Please, Mistress. I know I speak out of turn, but she is growing worse. Please, might you speak with Master Simon again? He is hurting her beyond bearing. When he brought her back today, she was only just beginning to awaken from a faint. She's never fainted before. He is only using her—"

"Enough!" Gloria approached the woman, her satin dress flowing around her like a river. Her every movement resembled a swan's graceful flight. "It is not your place to question your master's wishes, slave. What is your name once again?"

"Priscilla, Mistress," the slave woman said.

"Well, Priscilla, I will speak to Bianca myself. Go now."

Priscilla nodded gratefully. "Thank you, mistress," she said. She quickly left the room.

Gloria sank into an armchair before her vanity. Bianca always got in the way of her life. Gloria had been married to Simon for four years now. Bianca was a nuisance, a constant reminder of Gloria's own failings. She gave resources to her father that he desperately needed, and

Gloria could give Simon so little. Well, she would talk to the girl tomorrow. She would set things right.

A knock sounded on the chamber door. Certain knocks are so familiar that the person is known immediately. "Enter, Simon," Gloria said eagerly.

Simon glided into the room, his eyes alight. "I know where more jewels lie," he said. He approached the canopied bed and gazed down at his sleeping son. "His cheeks are flushed," he said. "Have you summoned the physician?"

Gloria shook her head. "His remedies are paltry," she said, approaching the bed as well. "Simon, I don't think the cures will ever—"

She stopped as she beheld his face. His smile had vanished completely. Gloria swallowed nervously. "I mean, the medicines seem to help Edward only for short periods of time. What if one day they no longer work at all?"

"I do not need you to lecture me," Simon said. "Do you not think I consider every possibility? Edward is my only son, the only child you were able to give me. I will do everything I can to keep him alive." He reached for Gloria's hand and drew her closer to him. "Do you doubt me, my treasure?"

Gloria's heart quailed as Simon's words invaded her mind. He did not mean to remind her of her inadequacies, of course, but he spoke truthfully. Edward caused Simon great worry, and his mysterious illness, which the physicians could not diagnose, was a financial burden.

Gloria could only blame herself for Edward's illness. She had given him life, after all, and he was always so near to death. But Simon must not become angry. He would go away again, and he rarely came to her as it was.

Gloria quickly shook her head. "Of course I don't doubt you, Simon. I just—It's just—Priscilla came to see me today." The final words emerged in a rush.

"What have I told you about problems concerning the slaves? I will deal with them myself," Simon said sharply.

"She said Bianca grows weaker and weaker each time you summon her. She said you brought her back today, and she was only beginning to awaken from a fainting spell. She's never fainted before. Simon, surely there must be some other way to find the jewels."

Simon thrust Gloria from him. "And why should a slave concern herself with my daughter?" he snapped. "I told you to make certain she does not associate with them! And there is no other way of making Edward well," he said. "She has the gift of hearing where the resources of our land lie. You know how badly the cotton crop suffered this year because of the boll weevils. I have to have means to obtain his medicine. Different remedies require more expensive ingredients. I am doing what is necessary to help him."

He turned to leave. "I came to deliver good tidings, but if you only want to complain—"

"No, Simon. Please stay." Gloria seldom resorted to begging, but he had not come to her in so long. She desperately needed his company. "I understand why you seek the jewels the land gives," she said. "I love Edward too. I'll try to make Bianca see reason. She's just so willful. Please, I'm trying my best."

She approached her husband and tentatively reached toward him. After a moment, he came to her. Simon bent close, gently kissing her. Gloria responded with eagerness, joy thrumming through her veins.

"Perhaps Bianca needs to regain her strength. Won't you consider only summoning her periodically?"

Simon nodded. "I'll consider it," he murmured. He drew Gloria even closer. When they drew apart, his smile had returned. "I'll take Edward to the nursery," he said breathlessly. "Then I'll come back. Please don't worry so, sweetheart. I'll take care of him."

Gloria nodded, relieved that Simon was here. There were times when his absences caused her great distress. Yet he always returned. She had to trust him.

CHAPTER THREE

e nter, Bianca." Gloria's voice was warm and inviting. Nervously, Bianca entered Stepmother's chamber. The room was opulent. Pearl-inlaid tables with many ornaments filled every available space. The high, vaulted ceiling resembled how Bianca imagined a cathedral might look. Of course, her own room was lavish as well, but she despised the chamber. So much luxury but still a prison. Stepmother seemed to be in her element, however.

Bianca approached the vanity table where Stepmother always sat. "You summoned me?" she asked.

Gloria smiled. "Yes, my dear. You mustn't be nervous. Sit." She gestured to a velvet-cloaked armchair. "I am having my breakfast. Would you like something?" She pointed to a tray of pastries and a pot of fragrant tea. "I can procure coffee for you. I never liked the taste myself."

Bianca shook her head and frowned. "I have already eaten." She gestured pointedly to the tray. "I helped Mabel assemble the breakfast you are eating, you know."

Gloria frowned for a moment. "Mabel? Oh, yes. Priscilla's daughter." She looked pointedly at Bianca, her eyes holding an indefinable expression. "Do you remember when you used to come to my chamber and admire my things? Do you remember the time I combed your hair?" She gestured to the combs and cosmetic caskets arrayed on her vanity table. "You told me you wanted to be as beautiful as me. I allowed you to use some of my cosmetics. Your cheeks shone so vibrantly."

Bianca fidgeted nervously. "Priscilla was angry with me. She said I was too little for cosmetics," she said. "I washed them off."

Gloria shook her head. "Of course Priscilla would be angry. After all, cosmetics could not conceal her blemish. Slaves are not fit—"

Her voice abruptly trailed away as she saw Bianca's angry expression. Gloria poured a liberal amount of milk into her teacup, and when she spoke again, her voice was brusque. "I understand your father summoned you yesterday. Are you feeling better this morning?"

Bianca nodded. "Still a bit tired, but the weakness always leaves me in a day or two." Her cheeks flushed with a smile. "We had a picnic. It was wonderful!"

Gloria frowned. How Edward would love picnics if he were only strong enough to go outside. "Yes," she said shortly. "I am glad to hear you had a good time." She leaned back in her chair. "How does the feeling come upon you?" she asked pensively. "Is it painful? What does the summoning of the land sound like?"

Bianca pursed her lips in thought. How did one describe something indescribable? "It's like at market when the merchants count their coins. A chinking, clattering sound. But it is not loud. It doesn't hurt my ears. It's as if the land is singing."

Gloria shook her head in confusion. "It does not hurt? Why, then, do you weaken so?"

"I don't know," Bianca said. "I just feel like I do after helping the slaves cook Sunday dinner: like a wet tablecloth is being pressed down on my head. I can't breathe."

Gloria rose and slowly approached Bianca. She bent forward, her eyes ablaze with earnestness. "This refusal of yours to stop spending time with the slaves is growing ridiculous. I have been more than indulgent with you. Please be sensible, child. They're inferior to you. The quicker you learn that—"

"That's not true!" Bianca cried. "And what am I supposed to do? You never have time for me, and Father—"

"My son takes priority!" Gloria snapped. Her face flushed with anger, and she blinked back tears. "Perhaps I should talk to Simon about procuring a tutor."

Bianca shuddered inwardly. A tutor would mean she must stop her lessons with Priscilla. She couldn't do that! But Stepmother did not know about their lessons. It was forbidden for slaves to read, but Priscilla had told Bianca that she had learned when she was a little girl. Bianca knew that no one could learn of this secret. She must not speak of it.

"Please, Stepmother. Why did you summon me?" she asked.

Gloria sighed. "I am concerned about this weakness you are experiencing. If your father summons you before two months' time, I want you to refuse to go with him." She held up her hand as Bianca opened her mouth to speak. "Your weakness will inhibit your ability to hear the singing of the earth."

"I want to go with him," Bianca said in surprise. "It's the only time I see Father. I'm Edward's only hope. I won't refuse Father's summons."

Gloria shook her head. "Even if the listening continues to weaken you?"

"I never stay weak long," Bianca said stubbornly. "I'll be all right."

Gloria's face hardened. "If I tell you to do something, you will do it. Do you understand? Yes, you are Edward's only hope of getting well, and that is the very reason I am giving you this order. Your duty is to be strong enough to listen, and after your fainting spell yesterday, I'm convinced that the next time you listen, something worse might happen. Your father is desperate to heal Edward, and his desperation is making him unreasonable. Edward is Simon's son, his favorite child," Gloria said bluntly.

She bestowed upon Bianca a long look, a look that spoke volumes. "You are old enough to know that a father in name only is not the same as one who loves you."

Bianca gasped, feeling as if she had been slapped. "How dare you? Father does love me!" she cried indignantly.

Gloria sighed, feeling guilt surface. "I meant that you must learn your place," she said. "Sons take precedence."

Gloria knew this fact only too well. Hadn't her own father been eager to be rid of her? Hadn't he insisted she marry the rich gentleman who wooed her, even though the courtship was a whirlwind affair? Fortunately, Gloria had grown to love Simon over the years, but there were times his brooding moods or bouts of anger frightened her. Her stepdaughter was naïve of the ways of the world. The sooner she awakened to reality, the better off she would be. But Bianca was so unreasonable!

Gloria turned away from the infuriating girl. "Go now," she said wearily.

136

Bianca rose and hurried to the chamber door. On the threshold, she turned and addressed Stepmother.

"You may look beautiful," she said flatly, "but you're ugly."

She fled the room, blinking back mercurial tears. Stepmother would not see her cry. The comment hurt so very much. It was a lie! At least, Bianca hoped that Stepmother lied.

Gloria's ears rang with the insult her stepdaughter had flung at her. In her mind, she saw Simon's furious face the day the physician had delivered the news that she could no longer bear children.

"You are weak. All you can give me is a sickly son!" he had fumed, his hand upraised. He had not struck her, but there was always the possibility he would.

Bianca needed to be strong in order to fulfill her purpose, but even a monthly summons hurt her. She had fainted yesterday, and that had never happened before. There had to be another way to procure what was needed to help Edward, a way that was more beneficial.

What if Bianca's gift could be used by someone else? Herself, for example? Gloria was a grown woman, and perhaps that meant she was stronger. Bianca's ability to hear where the land's resources were kept was a gift to be coveted. History books spoke of the rarity of such a gift. There were other books as well, books of forgotten lore that Gloria remembered perusing when she desperately sought any means to make her son well. She knew of a way to possess Bianca's gift, but her heart recoiled at the prospect. Even so, Gloria was desperate.

Gloria rang a bell beside her bed, and a slave girl entered the room.

"Bring Isaac to me," Gloria ordered. "I must speak with him."

CHAPTER FOUR

T he day began like any other. Bianca helped Priscilla assemble breakfast. Then she helped Mabel with the laundry. Of course, both Priscilla and Mabel told her not to help, but she had ignored them. Laundry was tedious, for each article of clothing and piece of linen had to be scrubbed repeatedly. The lye soap burned the hands and brought tears to the eyes.

"Mabel, do you ever feel—" Bianca was at a loss as to how to phrase her question. Ever since her visit with Stepmother, a feeling of disquiet worried at her soul like a dog at a bone. "Do you ever feel like you don't belong anywhere?"

Mabel looked up from the sheet she was scrubbing. Her sweat-soaked face wore a frown. "Every day," she said stiffly. "Why do you ask?"

"I just wondered. I feel like a piece of yarn that might break, like I'm being pulled in two directions. Father only summons me once a month, and I feel so tired after he does. But I love to see him. Stepmother only summons me to scold me. I only feel happy when I'm with all of you. But Stepmother said something mean yesterday." Bianca lowered her head. "I don't want to tell you what she said."

Mabel's face hardened. "I can guess," she said. She sighed and turned to Bianca. "Mistress, you know you don't belong among us, don't you? You'll only cause yourself trouble. Why do you keep coming back?"

Bianca sighed. "Because all of you make me feel welcome." She resumed her work. "Do you remember apple butter day last year?" she asked wistfully. That particular day always heralded fun for the slaves, for there were games and a picnic. The usual routines were set aside.

Mabel laughed, her features relaxing. "Next time, I'll beat you in the potato sack race." She laid aside the sheet and retrieved another article from the tub of water. "Do you remember the cakewalk? I know Isaac cheated." She laughed.

"He wouldn't!" Bianca said with a shocked gasp.

Mabel snorted. " 'Fly Along My Dovekin' isn't played that fast. Didn't you see him watching my mother? He wanted to make sure Mother stayed inside the circle and didn't step on the edge. She'd have been out if she had. Don't you remember how proud Mother was when she won the spice cake? It's her favorite."

Bianca laughed. She remembered Isaac's callused hands as they strummed the banjo and his weathered features that had smiled. He rarely played music or smiled, so that memory always made Bianca happy. "Priscilla sang that day," she said softly. "Her voice sounded so pretty." Bianca remembered the song:

Across the dividing river,
Amid wildflowers' golden gleam,
Lies a land bought by brutal means,
A land where we will go.

Bianca allowed the words of the song to fill her mind. They were mysterious, and she did not know what they meant, but they gave her comfort. She began scrubbing another article of clothing.

"Mistress Bianca?" Priscilla entered the washroom.

Bianca raised her head, shocked to see Priscilla's face. She was frowning, and tears shone in her eyes. "What is it?" She hurried to Priscilla's side.

Priscilla smiled wanly. "Isaac wants you to go with him today. He's selecting a pony for the stable. Mistress Gloria has given her permission. She said it was her final indulgence and that you must enjoy it."

Bianca gasped with excitement. "Really?" Another outing on the same week as the summons from Father? She looked at Priscilla's sad face, and suddenly her happiness evaporated like melting ice cream. "What's wrong?"

Priscilla shook her head. "Nothing, my dove," she said. "Go on out to the stable, now. He's waiting." She gave Bianca a quick hug. Bianca felt a cloth-wrapped bundle being placed in her hands.

"Provisions," Priscilla whispered. She hugged Bianca tighter.

"You're shaking." Bianca grabbed Priscilla's arm. "Please tell me—"

"Go." Priscilla thrust Bianca away, hastily turning to conceal her tears. "I'll tell you tonight during our lesson." She fled the room.

Bianca turned to Mabel. "I don't understand," she said.

Mabel shrugged. "Mistress probably yelled at Mother again. You know how it upsets her."

Bianca nodded. "Why don't you ask Isaac if you can come too?" she asked hopefully. "We could ask him to stop by the general store on the way home for some—"

Mabel shook her head. "I have to finish this washing," she said glumly.

Bianca sighed and nodded. Work always came first. She left the washroom to journey toward the stable.

Isaac ran his hands along Conrad's feet. The horse's shoes were worn, but they would suffice for the journey. He blinked rapidly as he saw Bianca hurrying toward him. "Morning," he said, managing a smile.

Bianca approached, her eyes shining. "Hello, Isaac. Thanks for asking me along."

He nodded. "You're always asking about the ponies at the stable yard. I thought you'd like to help me select one."

Bianca jumped up and down with excitement. "I hope they have a chestnut one," she said eagerly.

Isaac laughed. "Don't count your chickens," he said gruffly. "Come now. We'd best be going." He gestured to Conrad. "You'll ride behind me." He assisted Bianca onto the horse's back and mounted himself. "Did Priscilla pack you a lunch?"

Bianca nodded. "Can we stop at the general store for a dandy fizz on the way back?" she asked.

Isaac did not answer. After a moment, Bianca repeated her question.

"We'll see," Isaac said shortly. He pressed his heels into Conrad's sides, and the horse began to move. "I used to take you on rides when you were no bigger than a fledgling," he said.

Bianca looked at the man's weathered face. Faint memories stirred of glorious rides that took her breath away. She always felt like she was flying. "Did Father ever let me ride with him?" she asked.

Isaac frowned. "Not very often," he said. "He's a busy man, Mistress Bianca."

She lowered her head. "I was just thinking," she said. "I remember darkness and the smell of earth. It was cold, and I remember being on a horse with Father. We—"

"Stop talking about him!" Isaac said harshly. He yanked Conrad's reins, and the horse tossed his head in agitation.

Bianca flinched as if she'd been struck. "I'm sorry," she whispered. "I just—"

Isaac looked at the stricken girl, his face sorrowful. "Forgive me, Mistress Bianca. I didn't mean to yell," he said wearily. "You just don't understand. Your father is not—" He turned away and focused on guiding Conrad through a tangle of undergrowth. "So, do you feel stronger after the other day?"

"Yes," Bianca said, frowning at the abrupt change in subject. "It was just the usual weak spell. I have to learn to conserve my strength."

Isaac frowned. "It wasn't the usual weakness, Mistress Bianca. You fainted. And I don't think conserving your strength has anything to do with it. Seems to me that the weakness isn't your fault, contrary to what someone might want you to think," he said gruffly.

He continued guiding Conrad and did not speak again. He was not given to speaking as a general rule, so Bianca was used to his silences. She relaxed as Conrad continued cantering through the springtime landscape.

By midmorning, Bianca began to notice something strange. Trees surrounded her, and the temperature had fallen slightly. As they rode through the wood, the trees arched over her head in a graceful canopy. Silence surrounded her. Only the clip-clop of Conrad's hooves were discernible.

"Isaac, is the stable yard near?" she asked.

"We'll reach it by early afternoon. We'll eat before we arrive there," Isaac said.

After another hour or so of riding, Bianca was fidgeting uncomfortably. "I-I need to, um—"

Isaac nodded. "We'll stop in a moment." He spurred Conrad on. Even Bianca could tell that the horse was tiring. She noticed that Isaac gripped the reins in an iron fist.

Soon, the cheerful chattering of water filled Bianca's ears.

"Here," Isaac said, finally allowing Conrad to stop.

Bianca surveyed her surroundings. They had emerged in a sunny glade. A river bubbled just to the right of them, and wildflowers bloomed in abundance. Isaac turned to her. "Go do the necessary," he instructed. "Then we'll eat."

Bianca smiled at him. "It's beautiful here," she said as she dismounted from Conrad's back.

Isaac nodded. "My daughter and I used to come here," he said, a faint tremor in his voice. "Go now. I have to see to Conrad."

Bianca walked a stone's throw away in order to find some privacy. When she returned, Isaac was sitting on the grass eating a sandwich.

He turned to her. "I have sardines," he said, smiling faintly. "Would you like one?"

Bianca grimaced and shook her head decisively. "No thank you," she said haughtily. "I have my own lunch." She laughed as she opened the bundle of provisions. So much food for such a short journey!

As Bianca ate, she became aware of a strange noise. SNICK! SNICK! She turned toward the sound. Isaac was standing facing a tree, his lunch forgotten. He held something in his hand, something he was running along the tree's trunk. She saw that he was shaking, and tears were coursing down his cheeks.

"Isaac? Is something wrong?"

Isaac turned toward her, his right hand upraised. In his hand gleamed a knife.

"Run," he said, his voice barely recognizable. It emerged in a raspy growl. "Cross the river. You'll be safe if you reach the other side."

Bianca stared at Isaac, thunderstruck. The knife glimmered in his hand, the blade pulsating with evil itself. "What are you—"

He lunged toward her, knife blade sweeping in a deadly arc.

Bianca screamed and bolted toward the river like a frightened deer. Behind her, she heard Isaac's ragged sobs. Then she fell, the river catching her in its cold embrace. She tumbled head over heels. The current bore her along with insistent fingers, pushing her beneath the icy surface of the water. She knew no more.

CHAPTER FIVE

Mabel placed the tea service in the center of the table. The elaborate grandfather clock in the hallway struck the hour. Four o'clock. Why hadn't Bianca and Isaac returned? She straightened the cream pitcher.

"Mabel?"

The girl looked up from her work. Isaac had entered the dining room. Lines of weariness were carved onto his face. He carried a paper-wrapped package. Mabel shuddered when she saw the blood soaking through the paper. She was used to seeing Isaac with packages of meat, but the sight never failed to turn her stomach.

"Where's Priscilla? She's not in the kitchen."

"Mother's at the quarters in our cabin," Mabel said. "She has a headache."

Isaac nodded. "Mistress Gloria requested liver and onion stew for supper. I have the liver she wanted. I'll put it in the kitchen."

Mabel frowned. "We were going to make fried catfish."

Isaac shrugged. "Mistress' orders were for stew," he said flatly.

Mabel sighed. "I'll tell Mother." She finished arranging the tea things. "Is Bianca in the stable? What color pony did you get?"

Isaac turned around. She saw a muscle jump in his cheek. "Speak to Priscilla," he muttered. He hurried from the room.

"Isaac? What do you mean? What's wrong?" Mabel ran into the hall and stared after Isaac's retreating figure. Mistress Gloria would be down any moment. Well, she could ring the bell when she came. Something was wrong.

"Mirror, mirror, glass of fate, is Bianca in a place that is safe?" Priscilla clutched the ebony looking glass, her temples throbbing with fear.

The mirror, a gift from her own mother, showed her anything she needed to see. The mirror had once been ordinary, but her mother had made it extraordinary.

Priscilla thought of the boy who had scarred her face and of how, when she was grown, he had scarred her heart. He had taken her elder brother away to be sold along with other slaves. Priscilla thought of her despair.

"Stop your crying, child," Mother had said. "You know there's more to see in this world than your sorrow."

She had pointed to the ebony mirror on the cabin's makeshift table. "I asked the Creator to show me that my son was safe," she said. "He did so. This mirror can help you too." She gently touched the mirror's glass. "Mirror, mirror, shining with light, show my daughter more than her plight."

The mirror had opened up worlds of delights for Priscilla, particularly when it showed her the person she most wanted to see.

Now, Priscilla peered feverishly into the mirror's depths. "Please, Creator," she prayed. "Please protect Bianca."

A green-tinged mist caressed the glass. When the mist cleared, Priscilla gazed upon a log cabin. A young girl knelt on the ground. She wore a rough-woven tunic. Beside her lay a prone figure. Priscilla sucked in her breath as she beheld the tangled ebony hair and pale skin.

Bianca slowly sat up, her eyes wild with fear.

The girl placed her hand on Bianca's shoulder and spoke softly. "I was fishing with Papa and spotted you," she said. "You could've drowned."

"I—" Bianca coughed and tried to stand. "Where am I?"

The girl smiled. "Hart Spring," she said. "Bet you're freezing. Hungry, too. We're having fish chowder for supper."

The mirror darkened. Priscilla breathed a sigh of relief. Bianca was safe. Hart Spring was a sanctuary, and only the Creator could have guided Bianca there. His ways were so mysterious. Who else could have guided Bianca to the very house she needed to find?

Frantic knocking sounded on the cabin door. "Mother? I need to talk to you about Bianca."

Priscilla opened the door and admitted Mabel. Her daughter's face was drawn with concern.

"Is Mistress Gloria's tea ready?" Priscilla asked.

Mabel fidgeted impatiently. "Isaac says the mistress requested stew tonight," she said, getting to the point. "He left some meat in the kitchen. We were going to make catfish."

Priscilla nodded. It felt as if a hammer were pounding at her temples. "We'll save the fish for tomorrow night," she said.

"Do you know where Bianca is? I can't find her." Mabel looked into Mother's eyes, startled to see tears shining there. "What's happened?" She was suddenly frightened.

Priscilla tried to swallow the lump in her throat. "I cannot tell you, Mabel," she said. "Just know that Bianca's safe."

"Safe from what?" Mabel's heart pounded. "What's going on?"

"It's best that you don't know," Priscilla said firmly. "Go to the dining room and help Teresa. You know she's prone to dropping things. I'll join you shortly. I have to start supper."

Mabel sighed as she went to obey. It was useless to speak to Mother when she was in this type of mood.

Priscilla left her cabin and trudged to the great house. In the kitchen, she approached the counter. A wrapped parcel awaited her. Shaking, Priscilla unwrapped it. Inside lay the grisly trophy of a hunt. She trembled to think of the poor animal that had sacrificed itself for Bianca's sake. She began to prepare the evening meal.

CHAPTER SIX

Bianca placed a steaming spoonful of chowder into her mouth. She gazed around her at the wooden shelves, pewter utensils, and unadorned walls of the cabin. The surroundings reminded her of the slave cabin where Priscilla and Mabel slept. Yet this place didn't seem to be part of a plantation.

The man at the head of the table was staring at her with stern intensity. His burnished skin gleamed.

Hastily, Bianca put down her spoon. "Is something wrong?" she asked.

"You forgot about grace," the man said.

Bianca flushed. Grace was seldom spoken aloud at home. "I'm sorry," she said.

The man allowed his stern mask to slip a bit. "It's hard to resist Louise's fish chowder," he said gruffly. "I don't always wait for grace, either." He turned to where his daughter was sitting. "You forget sometimes too, don't you, Annika?"

Annika nodded unabashedly. "The Creator knows our thoughts, doesn't he?" she said, tossing her head. "He knows I'm thankful without my having to speak out loud."

The man laughed uproariously and snorted. "Good point, girl." He picked up his spoon and filled it to the brim.

"Honestly, you two!" A plump woman ambled from the back of the cabin carrying a cloth-wrapped loaf of bread. "Such talk!" She unwrapped the loaf and began cutting thin slices. She smiled at Bianca and chortled. "Don't mind my brood." She placed bread by Bianca's bowl. "No butter, I'm afraid."

Bianca smiled tentatively. "Thank you." She watched as the woman sat and pointedly bowed her head. Bianca followed suit. She couldn't restrain her laughter when Annika slowly lowered her spoon with an audible sigh.

"Great Creator, may you bless this food and reward the fish who gave themselves that we might partake," the father said.

"Amen," everyone chorused. The family ate.

After a moment, Bianca said, "This is delicious."

Louise smiled. "Why, thank you, my dear. It was my mother's recipe. The mistress and master whom George and I served loved—"

"Louise!" The man spoke harshly. "Now isn't the time."

"She has a right to know who we are, George," Louise said.

"Maybe so, but I'm sure she knows already. Let the girl at least get a hot meal inside her. We'll talk after that."

Bianca lowered her head in embarrassment. Of course she had had her suspicions, but she had feared to ask questions. Would they make her leave? She glanced at the man and woman. They did not seem angry. Maybe she was safe. She raised her head and continued eating. She noticed that Annika was staring at her with undisguised curiosity.

"You're pretty," Annika said shyly. "Are you royalty? You look like a princess."

Bianca's mouth flew open. "Royalty? Me?" She laughed. "No. I live on the plantation of Simon Reginald."

Annika gasped. "*The* Simon Reginald? The one who sent the slaves into the mine and it—"

"Enough!" George rose from the table, his face as grim as a storm cloud. "I'm going outside." He marched to the cabin door. "I'll be back in a moment."

When the door slammed behind him, Louise gave Annika a pointed look. "What have I said about being nosy?" she asked. "Go fetch some preserves."

Annika grinned. "Strawberry?" she asked.

Louise smiled. "Yes."

Annika skipped from the room. When she was gone, Louise said, "Don't let my husband worry you, child. He's harmless. And don't feel you have to answer any questions Annika asks."

Bianca pushed her empty bowl away. "I'm sorry to cause trouble," she said in a small voice. "Thank you for letting me stay the night."

Louise smiled. "You may stay as long as you like," she said. "Hart Spring is a place of refuge."

Bianca nodded. "I can help you with chores," she said.

"Here's the preserves." Annika skipped into the kitchen, holding a jar aloft.

The cabin door opened, and George came back inside. "No one is lurking about," he said gruffly. "I don't think anyone followed her." He sat at the head of the table and reached for the jar. "Storytime," he said unceremoniously.

Annika plopped onto the bench, her eyes shining. "We haven't had storytime in weeks!" she said excitedly. "Can our guest speak first?"

George frowned. "She doesn't know the routine. Let me start first so she won't be nervous."

Annika and Louise sat up straight. They continued eating as George spoke. "May I relate a tale?"

"Please do." Annika and Louise spoke together.

"Will you listen well?" George continued.

"Weave for us your word spell," Annika and Louise chorused.

"Creator, give my words grace," George said. "Let my tale enliven this place." He clapped three times.

Annika and Louise clapped four times. "Spin, spin, spin. Weave a tale of glory," they said.

Bianca gaped as she watched this strange ritual. She had never seen anything like it. Excitement filled her heart. It was as if she were experiencing something much bigger than herself.

George stood and began to speak. "When the world was new, the Creator gave the gift of his tears to the land. They were not tears of sadness, but tears of joy. His tears sank into the ground, where they hardened into sparkling jewels.

"The Creator loved all he had made. But, alas, men became prideful and greedy. Soon, they abandoned their Maker. Although they left him, he did not abandon them. His jewels remained, giving the land life.

"One day, a king began to savage the land. He took and took, wanting all the jewels for himself. The king had two children, a prince and a princess. The king ruled all with a voracious viciousness. He used men, women, and children to retrieve what he sought. The labor was hard, for the land did not want to yield its life source to someone so selfish.

"The princess felt empathy for those who were enslaved, but the king discovered where her loyalties lay and banished her from his kingdom.

"The prince, who was quite young, suffered greatly under his father's tyranny. When he assumed his father's throne, he resolved to be a strong ruler, one who would not be perceived as weak. So the harsh treatment of the slaves continued under the new king's rule. Many slaves died under his harsh treatment. As they retrieved jewels for their new king, the land collapsed around them. They knew something must be done.

"One night, a group of slaves fled into the darkness. As they walked along, they came to a river. They began helping each other across. But the king sent out his hunting hounds.

"As the slaves swam to the other side of the river, they heard blood-curdling howls as the hounds chased them. The slaves swam faster, but ever closer rang the menacing howls and pounding footfalls.

"Then the slaves saw a shimmer of white. A hart with gilded antlers stood in the path of the oncoming dogs. The dogs tore into the quivering animal, driving him to the ground. By the time the dogs had finished their evil work, the slaves had reached the other side of the river.

"The slaves found themselves in a different land. The king could not pursue them, for the hart was not what he seemed. He was the Creator in disguise. He wove a protection spell into the land.

"The slaves had fled in the spring of the year. To honor the Creator, the freed slaves named the land Hart Spring."

George finished his story. After a moment, Annika and Louise said, "Thank you for the tale you have spun."

"Thank you for listening," George said. He sat and turned to Bianca. The child's cheeks were flushed. "Do you have a story you would like to tell?" he asked gently.

Bianca blinked back tears. "Was that story true?" she asked. Priscilla's song filled her mind:

Across the dividing river,
Amid wildflowers' golden gleam,

Lies a land bought by brutal means,
A land where we will go.

George nodded. "All stories are true," he said. "I've simplified it, of course. Slavery has always existed in this world, and there are many masters. The country the slaves found was an exceptional place, a land where slavery was illegal. They sought asylum there and were granted it.

"Hart Spring is only one way the Creator works to help his people, you know. The Creator also imbues a precious few souls with gifts of sight and sound. Only a select few can see his tears, and fewer still can hear them singing. These gifted ones are responsible for keeping the land safe.

"You see, the Creator knows that the jewels are needed by those who suffer oppression. Those who can see and hear the jewels are responsible for finding trustworthy people who can help those in need. They can retrieve what is necessary to give to those who seek freedom. Many people travel here from far away, and they must have means of reaching this place. Sometimes that requires safe passage, and payment is needed."

Bianca placed her uneaten bread on the table. "I have a story," she whispered. "But it's unfinished. I can't remember how to start."

" 'May I relate a tale?' " Annika prompted.

Bianca repeated the words and then listened to the family's affirmative response. She asked the Creator to bless her words and began.

"There was once a queen who was unable to have children.

"One wintry day, as she sat sewing a maternity frock for a cousin who had already had three daughters, the queen pricked her finger. Drops of blood spattered onto the ebony windowpane, the drops of red intermingling with the sugary snow.

"The queen cried out in frustration. 'Creator, will you never hear my plea? If only I had a daughter with lips as red as blood, hair as black as ebony, and skin as white as snow!'

"After a time, the queen's prayer was answered. But, in giving birth to her daughter, the queen lost her life. There was no one to feed the girl, so she was placed in the care of a slave woman with a scarred face. The woman was the girl's wet nurse. As the girl grew, she worked with the other slaves, never seeing her father. She only felt at home among the wet nurse and her people.

"When the girl was eight years old, the king married again. The stepmother was kind but distant. When she had a son of her own, the queen neglected her stepdaughter. The queen's son was often ill. The girl loved her stepbrother and would often prepare for him treats she hoped would give him strength: oatmeal dripping with honey, egg custard, and many other delights. When the boy was strong enough, she would talk to him and he would talk to her.

"When the girl was nine, her father summoned her. He took her to a dark cave and told her to look around her. The girl obeyed even though the darkness frightened her. 'I see nothing but dirt and rocks,' the girl said. The king looked at her with sad disappointment, the look of a child who has been denied a sweet after supper. He turned away from her, and the girl felt so alone.

"Frantically, she looked about her once more. There was nothing to see, but she suddenly discovered there was something to hear. The cave rang with a beautiful music. 'I hear singing!' the girl cried excitedly. 'Father, I hear singing!' She longed to please her father. Perhaps then he would tell her he loved her and would spend more time with her.

"As the girl listened to the music, she realized that the earth was calling to her. It told her that much treasure lay underground. She told her father this news, and he smiled and embraced her. He no longer looked disappointed, but thrilled. 'Very good, sweet princess,' he said. 'You will make my son well. You will give me so much.'

"The girl promised to try. However, the more she listened to the earth, and the more her father took its jewels, the weaker the girl became.

"One day, her father's manservant took the girl into the forest. He drew a knife and told her to run. He told the girl she would be safe if she crossed a nearby river."

Bianca finished the story, and the family solemnly thanked her for the tale.

After a moment, Louise said, "You poor dear." She reached for Bianca's hand.

Bianca relaxed. The family would keep her safe. In return, she would do what she could to thank them.

CHAPTER SEVEN

G loria paced in her chamber. Her stomach roiled with nausea. When would she hear the earth's cry? Would Simon hear it too? He had eaten heartily at supper, even making a point to send his compliments to the kitchen. Gloria had eaten moderately, each mouthful tasting of ashes.

I am doing this for Edward, she reminded herself. Would the gift manifest itself quickly, or would it take time? Would she become as weak as her stepdaughter had?

Simon's familiar knock sounded. Gloria eagerly admitted him. "Are you well, darling?" she asked anxiously.

Simon frowned. "Of course I am," he said. "Why wouldn't I be?" He approached her, and they embraced. "Edward's medicine will be ready tomorrow," he continued. "Three bottles' worth. I sold a triple amount of Hart's Tears today, so I asked the pharmacist to make the medicine even stronger. Edward will be all right. I'll go to the drugstore tomorrow and collect it."

Gloria smiled. She breathed a sigh of relief. "Will he live, Simon?" she whispered. "Please tell me he'll live."

Simon leaned toward her. "I won't let him die. You know that," he said. "My treasure, you must trust me." He kissed her passionately.

Mabel washed dishes in the kitchen. She wondered where Bianca could be. She was always quick to tell Bianca she must not help her, but, truthfully, she missed the companionable conversations they shared.

Mabel ceased her work and hung her head. In addition to her worry, she felt oddly fatigued. She had fed Edward supper (a task Bianca usually insisted on performing) and had been weary ever since. A sweet scent had filled the nursery, one that she could not place. But Edward needed sustenance, and she loved him just as much as Bianca did.

Mother passed by Mabel with a pile of clean napkins. "Your supper's in the pantry," she said over her shoulder.

Mabel nodded her thanks. After she completed her work, she hurried to the pantry.

"You saw her?" Isaac's voice trembled. "She's all right?"

Mabel turned toward the voices. Mother and Isaac were folding napkins and speaking earnestly. Mabel knew she shouldn't eavesdrop, but curiosity nagged at her.

"She's in Hart Spring," Mother said. Tears shimmered in her eyes. "You will find this hard to believe, but she's with George's family."

Mabel watched as Isaac bowed his head. "The Creator be praised," Isaac breathed. "I'm sorry, Priscilla. I had to do it. That woman must be mad. Did she really think I would bring her a child's liver?"

Priscilla frowned. "Edward grows weaker every day," she said. "Mistress is mad with desperation, I think. That pig of a man manipulates—" She turned her face away, raising a hand to cover her scar. Finally, she said, "What animal did you use to fool her?"

Isaac grimaced. "A deer."

Mabel dropped the corn bread she was holding. Her ears rang. No! This wasn't true! Hart Spring was just a story, wasn't it? A fairy tale that gave false hope. What had happened to Bianca?

CHAPTER EIGHT

"Where is she?" Simon stood before Priscilla, his hands on his hips. His face was flushed with rage. "When I summon my daughter, I expect her to come to me."

Priscilla looked up from the bread dough she was kneading. "You'd do best to ask your wife, Master," she said flatly.

Simon stared at her. "I know she often comes here," he said. "And have I not warned you repeatedly to send her away when she does? You dare to defy—"

"I dare nothing. I'm simply telling you the truth." She bestowed upon him a penetrating gaze. "But you refuse to see anything that doesn't benefit you."

Simon sneered at her. "I could have you whipped for speaking to me in this way," he said. He gazed pointedly at her scarred face. "But of course you know that, don't you?"

Priscilla slammed her fists into the mound of dough. "How could whipping be any worse than what you've already done?" Her voice caught in her throat. "You sold my brother on the auction block. You use Bianca until she's weak beyond bearing. I know it is foolish for me to think I have any right to that girl. After all, why should someone who has given a baby her own milk feel anything for her? You think yourself so superior to me! I have feelings, Master. At least your sister understood."

Simon raised his hand as if to strike her. Then he slowly lowered it. A strange smile crossed his features. "My sister was foolish, and you took advantage of that, didn't you? You don't think I know that it was she who had the audacity to teach you to read? I could have told my father, you know, but I found other ways to punish you." He smiled. "I can hurt you beyond bearing. Tell me where my daughter is. I need more medicine for Edward."

Priscilla stared at him in shock. "It's only been a week," she said. "Surely you have enough medicine to last for at least a month. Isaac drove you to the drugstore only seven days ago."

Simon turned from her in disgust. He had to have the jewels. They were the only thing that gave him confidence. For a moment, he thought of his bedchamber and the secret that lay within it. He thought of his sister's tears.

"It's none of your concern," he said. He stormed from the room.

Priscilla set the bread to rise and hurried to her cabin. She retrieved her mirror. "Mirror, mirror, gleaming with light, show me the child in his nursery bright." She knew that something was wrong.

The mirror glowed greenly, then cleared. The little boy sat amid an array of toys on the nursery floor. He moved a stuffed lion and bear across the floor, roaring, growling, and grinning.

Suddenly, Edward grew still. He looked toward the ceiling of his nursery.

A mobile swayed lazily back and forth. The trinket was carved from applewood and depicted a dragon capturing a princess. The dragon's sinewy tail was wrapped around the princess' waist. The princess was beautiful. A bejeweled comb nestled in her flowing hair.

As the mobile swung to and fro, the air seemed to thicken. Edward gazed transfixed at the dazzling decoration. Then he fell backward onto the floor. His eyes closed in sleep. His cheeks flushed with fever.

Priscilla placed the mirror on the table. What was the meaning of this? One moment, the boy was fine. The next—

The cabin door burst open. Gloria swept into the room, her eyes wild.

"You!" She pointed an accusing finger at Priscilla. She was shaking. "What did you do with them? Where are they?"

Priscilla calmly observed her hysterical mistress. "With what?"

"Edward's bottles of medicine. Where did you hide them, you worthless—"

"I don't know what you mean, Mistress."

Gloria sneered with contempt. "Don't you? You've always thought of yourself as Bianca's mother. You did this for vengeance."

Priscilla blinked. "I love Edward. I would never harm him. The Creator knows I'd love to make you suffer, may he forgive me, but I could never hurt a child."

"Then how do you explain three bottles of medicine disappearing? Simon told me only tonight that they were gone."

She stared around the makeshift room and rushed to the table by which Priscilla stood. "Are they here?" Gloria frowned as her eyes fell on the mirror. "What is this?" She snatched the looking glass and peered into it. "Is this some trinket you obtained by selling my property? Where's the medicine, slave? Tell me, or I'll have you beaten to within an inch of—"

Gloria's tirade stopped as the mirror began to reveal a picture. "Simon's bedchamber? What's the meaning of this?" she whispered.

Priscilla cautiously approached the table. "May I see?"

Gloria sank to her knees, letting the mirror fall from her limp grasp. She began to keen, the sound resembling a tortured animal.

Priscilla retrieved the mirror. Within its reflection, she saw what she had been afraid she would see. She tentatively reached for her mistress' hand.

The glass showed an opulent bedchamber with crimson hangings and many portraits. One portrait hung at the back of the chamber and dominated all: the picture of an imposing-looking man with a hard face and an upraised hand. Priscilla knew that portrait. The picture depicted Master Simon's late father.

As Priscilla stared at the room, the portrait seemed to open like a door. She saw that the picture's frame was not completely affixed to the wall. A portion could be moved, and the whole picture could then swing outward.

Behind the portrait, a smaller chamber appeared. A single set of shelves was the only furnishing in the smaller room. The shelves gleamed with the brightness of decorated boxes. The wooden containers were adorned with filigree, but the boxes' outward adornments were nothing compared to what gleamed inside them. Jewels shone within the boxes, a veritable treasure trove.

One shelf held only a plain item: a bottle with a skull and crossbones symbol upon it.

CHAPTER NINE

Bianca scrubbed the cabin floor. Annika followed behind her, pretending to clean but really only making sudsy curlicues in the water.

"I liked your story last night," Bianca told the girl. She grinned. "That hedgehog sounded like a wonderful pet."

Annika laughed. "Prickles was," she said happily. "Papa was mean to make me turn him loose, though."

Bianca shook her head. "Prickles was wild. He didn't want to live in a cabin. He wanted to be free."

Annika sighed. "I would have made him a place outside." She grinned at Bianca. "Mama and Papa will be home from market soon. I hope the dandy fizz man will be there!"

Bianca laughed. "You like dandy fizz too?"

"Yes! It dances, and it makes me burp."

"You're too much, Annika!" Bianca tickled the girl under the chin. Annika squealed with delight. "Now help me cook supper. How do potato pancakes and apple butter sound? I think there's some leftover chowder too."

Annika grinned. "I want the biggest pancake." The two companions began their work.

Bianca had been with Annika and her family for only a week, but she felt stronger than she had in some time. Hart Spring was a true sanctuary, and she was grateful to have been led to it. But she often thought of her family across the river. She missed Mabel and Priscilla. She even missed Isaac. And she could not help thinking of Father. What if Edward had grown weaker because of her neglect? He needed her help, and she was hiding away.

George and Louise entered the cabin. They held sacks of provisions. "Greetings, girls," Louise said cheerfully. "They had so many things at market today. The cheese lady was there, and—"

"The dandy fizz man! Was he there?" Annika asked eagerly.

"You'll see." George smiled when he saw the jar of apple butter on the table. "It's been awhile since I tasted that," he said. "Didn't think we had any in the pantry."

Bianca smiled at him, and everyone prepared to eat.

When supper was finished, Louise rose to clear the table. "You girls worked hard all day," she said. "I'll clean up."

George looked at Louise with a pointed stare. "I shared a story the first night our guest arrived," he said. "Annika related her tale last night. I think it's time we heard one from you."

Louise sighed. "You're the better storyteller, George. You should tell it."

"She needs to know how we arrived here," George said gently. "And I think this story is best told by you."

"Oh, please don't think you have to explain," Bianca said hurriedly. "It's all right."

Louise and George exchanged somber looks. Finally, Louise sat down. "May I relate a tale?"

Bianca couldn't help smiling as she joined the family in their responses to Louise's questions. The ritual was becoming an event she loved dearly, a delightful way to feel as if she belonged and was wanted. She listened as Louise told her story.

"There was once a husband and wife who worked on the plantation of a kind master and mistress. Well, as kind as people can be who own human beings. They did not whip their slaves, and they sought to make them as comfortable as they could. Anyhow, the wife had been born on the plantation. She had served as wet nurse to the mistress' youngest son when her own child had been born dead.

"As the years passed, the plantation fell onto hard times, and the master was forced to make a decision. He needed money to pay mounting debts, so he decided to sell most of his slaves and just keep enough to maintain the plantation. Everyone knew what selling meant, particularly the wife's husband. He himself had been sold when he was a younger man. Master promised not to split families apart, but auctions were unpredictable. Children were often taken from their mother's arms, and husbands and wives were often separated, never to see each other again.

"A week before the auction was to take place, the mistress summoned the wife to her chamber. She handed the wife a pouch of money. 'I want you to go to the general store for me tomorrow,' the mistress said. 'I want you to buy some molasses and coffee.' She gave the wife a folded cambric handkerchief, adorned with embroidery. 'Give this handkerchief to the store clerk. It is a gift for his wife. Her name is Janet.' The wife said she would carry out her mistress' instructions.

"The next day, the wife went to the store to purchase the items. The clerk smiled at her kindly. She handed him the handkerchief. The clerk unfolded the cloth. The wife knew it was wrong to look, but she could not resist. She leant forward. On the handkerchief was an embroidered picture of two clasped hands, the hands of a man and woman. Their hands rested on the majestic crowned head of a hart. What could this strange picture mean? The wife wondered.

"The clerk looked at the wife. 'There is a place called Hart Spring where slaves have found freedom.' He smiled as he stroked the delicate handkerchief. His voice grew soft. 'I can drive you and your husband to the river in my carriage, but you must cross the river yourselves. I will have a lantern and will remain on that side of the river to see you cross safely. Do you want to go there?'

"The wife was shocked, but hope filled her heart. She felt the familiar stirring in her belly, the reminder that her child was growing within her. Her child could be born free. There would be no danger of the auction block.

"She raised her head and smiled at the clerk. 'I accept your offer of assistance,' she said.

"All went according to plan. That night, the general store clerk came to the plantation with a sack of coffee that he claimed the wife had forgotten. The husband and wife met him a stone's throw away from the plantation, and he drove them to the river. They crossed the river safely and have lived in Hart Spring ever since. Their little girl was born five months after their arrival."

Louise nodded, indicating that her story was done. The family thanked her for her tale, and she thanked them for listening.

After a moment, Bianca asked, "Do you think the mistress and the store clerk were punished?"

Louise bowed her head. Finally, she said, "I do not know, but I think it wouldn't have mattered to them if they had been." She wiped tears from her eyes. "Some people are born with courageous spirits. They'll help those in need for common decency's sake. One day, I would love to give my mistress this." She withdrew a handkerchief from her tunic and unfolded it. "I made this myself."

She handed the handkerchief to Bianca. On the delicate cloth were embroidered three doves. They were not caged. Beneath them stood a hart, his head held high as a regal king. He appeared to be watching the doves' joyous flight of freedom.

Bianca smiled. She rose to her feet and gave Louise a hug. Then she turned to George. "I'm sorry you were sold when you were young," she said softly.

George nodded. "I have to remind myself that mysterious things happen every day," he said gruffly. "Perhaps my sister will find me one day." He laughed. "Priscilla's quite tenacious. If anyone can find freedom—"

He broke off as he beheld Bianca's shocked face. He smiled at her. "Thought you'd recognize that name," he said.

CHAPTER TEN

Mabel was preparing Edward's supper. The boy was so weak he could barely lift his head. He could only manage small sips of broth. Even so, he needed as much sustenance as possible.

Mabel lifted the tureen and slowly walked to Edward's nursery. She opened the door and went inside. Edward lay on his bed. He was very still. Mabel's heart skipped a beat. Was he—No, Creator be thanked! He was breathing.

Mabel hurried to the bed and lifted the child's head. "Wake up, Master Edward. You need strength," she said soothingly. "It's vegetable broth." She spooned soup into the child's mouth. Most of it dribbled down Edward's chin, but he managed to swallow a few drops.

CHING! CHING!

Mabel looked up. A strange decoration hung from the ceiling. It swayed back and forth. A princess writhed in the coils of a dragon. The comb she wore swayed with the movement of the decoration. The dragon and the princess were entwined in an eternal dance. Their gyrations created a strange, hypnotic music. As the comb swayed in the princess' hair, Mabel noticed that tiny rivulets of crimson billowed in the air and dispersed, similar to the way dandelion seed was borne upon the breeze. Was the ceiling in need of dusting? A faint fragrance filled the room. The scent was indescribable, a mixture of apples and vanilla.

"Do you like it?"

Mabel spun around, the tureen wobbling in her hands. Master Simon had entered the room without her hearing him. "It's custom made," he continued. "I bought it from a travelling peddler. It's impressive, isn't it?"

Mabel cleared her throat. "Yes, Master. I-it's lovely."

"Indeed." Simon's smile broadened. "You're Priscilla's daughter, aren't you?"

Mabel nodded.

"Very good." He pointed to the mobile once again. "Your mother called me a dragon once. She was very young then, as was I. The words stung at the time, but now I recognize them for the compliment they were." Simon leant toward her. "I need your help. What's your name, girl?"

Mabel longed to step away from his intense stare. "M-Mabel. My name is Mabel."

Simon nodded. Slowly, he reached into his pocket and withdrew a bottle with a strange symbol. From another pocket, he produced a handkerchief, which he held to his nose. He sauntered to the swaying decoration and removed the comb from the princess' hair. Carefully, he poured a small quantity of crimson powder into the rectangular cavity that was revealed. As if dressing royalty, Simon placed the comb back into the princess' flowing tresses. For a moment, his face convulsed. Was he angry or sad? Mabel could not tell.

Simon placed the bottle back into his pocket. "I knew a girl like you once. She was my sister. She was so joyful, so full of life. But she made a choice to associate with the weaklings of the world, and she was beaten for her decision." He gazed down at his hands and flexed them. Mabel saw that his hands shook.

"My father caught her and five slaves as they were leaving the plantation one night. Janet carried a purse of stolen jewels from Father's bureau drawer. I was twelve when this happened.

"Father told me it was time that I proved myself a man. He stood over me while I administered ten lashes across my sister's back. He paid me for the deed with Hart's Tears from the very purse that Janet had stolen. The slaves were forced to watch Janet's punishment. That was when your mother called me a dragon. I was so angry! I hit her face with the whip. What does she know of anything? Do you know that the only time Father ever said he was proud of me was that night?"

Simon sighed and shook his head. "Not that it matters. People abandon you and care nothing for you. That's the reality of this world. Only rely on the material things, the things that give you security. Janet abandoned me, you know."

His voice had grown conversational, and a strange gleam danced in his eyes. "Slaves tended to her wounds, and I haven't seen her since that fateful night. She left the comforts of home to wallow in the mire." He laughed harshly. "She thinks she is strong, but she is weak. Who is living with riches, and who must struggle to maintain even a semblance of life? Last I heard, she was married to a common store clerk."

He inclined his head toward Mabel, who had turned toward the door. "There are many dragons in this world, girl, and do you know who causes the fire within them to smolder? Every chattel who has the gall to think herself superior to her betters. Your mother was instrumental in causing my sister to betray her family. Janet is a fool! Did she honestly think that girl would even remember her after she escaped? She would only have used her. Priscilla tends to forget her place on occasion. You'll help her to remember, won't you?"

He smiled as he turned his attention back to the mobile. "Dragons are strong and always consume their prey, you know. Oh, occasionally someone escapes them, but so many do not." He turned back to her.

Mabel took a step toward the door, and Simon raised a hand, gesturing for her to stop. "So anxious to leave my company? I have not dismissed you." His voice was as gentle as ever, but Mabel had never felt so frightened.

Mabel wanted to run, but her feet felt rooted to the ground. Simon reached toward her and gently took the tureen from her hands, placing it on a table. "You work hard, my dear. You need a good night's rest. I'll send your mother to fetch you." He gathered Edward into his arms. Simon glided from the room, closing the door behind him.

The apple perfume assailed Mabel's nostrils, its scent no longer faint but overpowering. She choked on the cloying aroma. The room was so very hot! She staggered toward the door but could not move quickly enough. She collapsed. Above her head, the mobile swung to and fro, to and fro, singing a lullaby of doom.

In her cabin, Priscilla screamed. The door opened as she was bolting to her feet.

"I never fancied I'd find you so quickly." Simon sauntered into the cabin and gazed around him in disgust. "I remember the day I summoned your brother from here," he said. "Your mother was quite the fighter, wasn't she? But her attack proved futile. I still got what I wanted. The world is divided into the strong and the weak, and we both know who was strongest, don't we? He fetched a handsome price at auction." He smiled at her. "It seems you already know what has transpired concerning your daughter. Mabel, is it? I would be very much interested in knowing how you learned of her predicament." He approached Priscilla and stared at the mirror clutched in her shaking hand. "A trinket of some sort, eh?"

Priscilla glared at him. "You know what it is."

"Indeed." Simon's smile faded. "Your mother gave it to you as a gift. It's the same mirror in which she claimed to see my future." He sighed. "Ignorance is a blissful state. I used to know so little. Then I learned the truth. You fail to realize that without me and others like me, you and all your kind could not survive. Are you not sheltered and clothed? You are expected only to give what is due in return. I remember when you married. Such a shame your happiness with your husband was short-lived. The mine collapse was an unfortunate accident, of course," he said. "I do regret the death of the little girl."

Priscilla sucked in her breath as she thought of her husband and the accident at the mine that had claimed his life and the lives of so many others. She thought of Isaac's daughter. "Heidi was only five," she whispered. "Isaac's wife died from grief. You truly think obtaining the jewels from the mines is worth the disasters you cause?"

Simon languidly reached for the mirror. Priscilla tried to hold it out of reach, but his hands closed over the ebony handle. He smiled as he gazed at the image before him: the image of a girl lying prone on the ground. "Apple toxicant is quite easy to obtain. The seeds themselves contain the toxin. I have added opium to the formula. It helps a person sleep while the apple toxicant does its work. Despite what you think of me, I do not desire to cause pain. But enough of the poison will inhibit breathing. I advise you to tell me what I want to know and quickly. Where is my daughter?"

Priscilla lunged, grabbing Simon's wrist. "Your daughter's name is Bianca!" she hissed as she viciously yanked his arm. "I hope Mother's vision about your future comes true. I hope your death is painful. I hope your son grows up to be stronger than you." She released his arm and smiled as she saw the mirror crash to the floor. As the glass shattered, she caught the fleeting glimpse of a log cabin. Bianca was outside folding laundry.

Simon snarled in fury. "Tell me where that cabin lies," he said. "Tell me, or I'll obtain a poison far more painful. Mabel will die in agony."

Priscilla bowed her head in defeat. "Hart Spring," she whispered. "Bianca is in a community called Hart Spring."

I'm such a fool! Gloria sat at her vanity and peered into her looking glass. Her features were ravaged. What she had seen in the slave woman's mirror couldn't possibly be true, could it? Surely Simon had been procuring medicine for his son all this time. Surely he loved Edward as much as she did.

Gloria's chamber door opened, and Isaac entered the room. His features were carved from granite. "Your son's in danger, Mistress," he said without preamble. "Where is he?"

Gloria pointed a quivering finger to her canopied bed. "He's here. Simon brought him here earlier this evening. Edward was here when I returned from the slave quarters." She swallowed convulsively. "Do you know where Simon is now?"

Isaac bowed his head with sadness. "He's preparing to journey to a place called Hart Spring," he said. "That's why I came to you. I must take Edward away from here."

Gloria frowned. "What is Hart Spring?"

"It's a community," Isaac said. "Runaway slaves have established a settlement in a neighboring country where slavery is prohibited. The people of Hart Spring have their own governing authorities. Hart Spring is where Bianca is now." He stared pointedly at Gloria's pale visage. "Surely you knew that I couldn't kill an innocent child."

Gloria looked at him for a long moment. "Perhaps I did," she whispered. "I simply don't know what I was thinking. I just wanted to help my son. Do you know how hard it is to watch someone wither before your eyes, someone whom you have given life? I could do nothing for him. Perhaps I sought Simon's attention as well." She laughed bitterly. "Fool that I am." She bowed her head in defeat.

"There's an old custom of taking the essence of someone into yourself," she continued, her voice shaking. "Edward's so ill. I thought if I took Bianca's gift, then I could hear where the jewels lay buried in the mines. I-I thought I could help Simon to hear as well."

Her voice trailed away. She thought of Simon's upraised hand and how she so desperately longed to please him. She thought of his anger at Edward's many bouts of sickness as an infant. Gloria raised her head and looked into Isaac's eyes. "I could have hired someone to kill Bianca, you know, someone who would have done the job without remorse. Perhaps you know me better than I know myself. I'm not a complete fool. I know how much you love her."

She turned to her sleeping son and stared at him for a long moment. When she turned back to Isaac, her voice

179

was strong. "Do what you must."

Isaac approached the bed and gently gathered the sleeping boy into his arms. "I will find the place where Bianca is staying," he said. "The family there will take care of Edward until it's safe for him to return." He frowned. "Simon will pursue us. If I could buy some time, we might reach Hart Spring before he does."

Gloria nodded. She went to her vanity and opened the bottom drawer. Withdrawing a small bottle from the drawer, she handed it to Isaac. "It's a syrup of poppy and mandragora," she said. "I cannot sleep at night, and the physician has prescribed this. Take it and do what you have to do." She managed a weak smile. "Simon loves apple butter. He's been known to eat it straight from the jar."

Isaac smiled at her. "There's only one jar left in the cellar." He turned to the door. "You place your life in danger by helping me," he said.

"I will protect my son at all costs," Gloria said flatly.

Isaac bowed his head. "I know how it feels to lose the ones you love," he said. "I'll take care of Edward as if he were my own. If you decide to join us, Hart Spring lies to the north across a river. Look for the hand in the sky, the hand that holds a drinking cup." He left the room.

Gloria gazed at the closed door in shock. She had never been kind to the slaves, yet they were helping her son. They were offering her help as well. How was that possible?

Gloria rang her bell. "Simon leaves for a journey tonight," she said to the girl who entered the room. "Pack a basket of food for him. There's a jar of apple butter in the cellar. It's the last one. Be certain to pack it. It's his favorite. Let me know when he prepares to leave."

The slave girl nodded. "Yes, Mistress."
Gloria sat at her vanity to wait.

CHAPTER ELEVEN

Tell me she'll live." Priscilla stood in the stable, Mabel cradled in her arms.

Isaac solemnly placed his fingers on Mabel's neck. He breathed a sigh of relief. "There's a pulse," he said. "But it's very faint." He gestured to a lantern on the ground. "We must go." He gently took Mabel from Priscilla's arms and turned to the wooden cart behind him. The conveyance was a makeshift contraption of weathered wood with rickety wheels. It was used by field slaves to haul produce to the barn. "She'll ride in this beside Edward."

Priscilla nodded. She reached for the lantern. "I'll carry that."

Isaac shook his head. "No. We'll hang it on the side of the cart. I need your help to pull it." He glanced at the wheels, which he had wrapped in burlap. "The cart will be quieter," he said gruffly, "but not much." He glanced inside at Mabel and Edward, who lay motionless. "Creator be with us," he breathed. He gestured for Priscilla to join him at the front of the cart. They headed into the night.

Outside, the stars shone with brilliance, dancing their constant praise. When Isaac and Priscilla looked at them, they realized how small they themselves really were.

"There," Isaac whispered reverently, pointing northward.

A group of stars stood still. The outline of a steady hand pointed ahead, its fingers slightly bent as if it cradled a drinking cup. Beams of clear light emanated from this constellation as if the cup's liquid were being poured out as refreshment for all who would partake.

"We must follow the drinking cup," Isaac said.

As the companions trudged along, Priscilla said, "I had to break Mother's mirror. He'd have taken it if I hadn't."

Isaac nodded. "Your mother was a wise woman in every sense of the word," he said solemnly.

Priscilla smiled. "She told me that if Simon ever tried to take the mirror, I was to break it."

"Do you think her vision about Simon will come true?" Isaac bowed his head as Priscilla's mother's words about Heidi filled his mind. " 'A noble maiden will give her life to satisfy a dragon's greed,' " he whispered. "Heidi had the smallest hands and could reach into crevasses others could not. One day, we were digging as frantically as we could while he waited outside. That's when the collapse happened." He choked on a sob.

Priscilla nodded sadly and gazed at Isaac with tender concern. " 'A dove's tears will vanquish our fears, and a boy will grow up to become stronger than his father,' " she said softly. "I have to believe Mother's visions, Isaac. I'd die if I didn't. We have to believe, and we have to fight, or we are nothing."

Isaac bowed his head. "I know. Do you remember when Sarah and I tried to run? We were caught." He trembled as the memories assailed him. "Sarah was chained to an oak tree with her arms stretched to either side of her. Her back was bare. M-Master Simon forced me to whip her. He said whipping was too tame a punishment for me, that my punishment would scar my heart and not my back." Isaac allowed the tears to come freely. "All the field slaves were forced to watch."

He stared at Priscilla for a long moment. "I know we have to keep fighting, Priscilla, but I'm so tired."

Priscilla nodded. She gazed at Isaac. She did not speak, but her silent empathy was enough. The journey continued, and the darkness thickened around them. Crickets serenaded the travelers, and a rousing breeze tousled their hair. The breeze carried the scent of springtime.

Suddenly, Priscilla held up her hand and gasped. "Stop, Isaac," she whispered. "Look." There was movement in the cart. Mabel fidgeted.

"The Creator be praised!" Priscilla gasped as Mabel slowly opened her eyes.

Mabel felt the caress of a welcome breeze. What a relief that the cloying scent had vanished! Why was the ground shaking? She felt a jarring sensation. Mabel slowly sat up.

"Mother?" she whispered.

Priscilla knelt on the ground, tears of relief coursing down her cheeks. She soothed Mabel with a caress. "I'm here, sweetheart, and so is Isaac," she reassured the girl. "We're taking you somewhere safe. Edward is with us too."

Mabel turned, shocked to see Edward lying beside her on a cart of some kind. "Where are we going?" Her heart quailed in fear as she thought of Master Simon. "Will he try to find us?"

Isaac nodded. "He'll not be far behind," he said bluntly. "I pray I've managed to buy enough time." He pointed to the north. "We're going to Hart Spring. You've heard the story of the free community?"

Mabel frowned. Vague recollections surfaced of a fairy tale about a hart facing a pack of hunting hounds as frantic slaves swam across a river to freedom. "It's just a story," she said.

Priscilla smiled. "A story that reflects the truth." She bowed her head in reverence. "We must always remember those who were left behind. So many stay so that others might run." Her voice broke.

Finally, she said, "Can you walk, sweetheart? We must go on."

Mabel tentatively stood. Her limbs shook with weakness, but she managed to walk. "When we reach Hart Spring, will we be free?" she asked.

Priscilla nodded. "Indeed we will," she said. "But I fear it will not happen without much pain."

"Look," Isaac said suddenly. "The boy's stirring."

CHAPTER TWELVE

Where was Isaac? Simon surveyed the kitchen and the hallway. He had to be on his way. Retrieving his daughter would be simple now that he had discovered her whereabouts. He sighed with impatience.

"You." He gestured to a slave girl who was passing. "Go to the quarters and find Isaac for me. I must travel tonight. Bring me my provisions."

The girl hurried to obey. When a basket was handed to him, Simon left the house to walk to the stable.

The stable was empty, and Simon sat on a bale of hay to wait. Where was the confounded man? To pass the time, he perused the basket of food. Simon smiled as he saw the small jar of apple butter. He opened the jar and began to eat, slathering gargantuan amounts onto slices of bread.

"You're nothing but a pig."

Simon raised his head at the familiar voice. Gloria stood framed in the doorway. She was pale, and her eyes swam with tears. "Was there ever a time that you loved him, Simon?"

Simon blinked in confusion. "What are you doing out here, woman?" he asked. "What's the meaning of—"

"I saw the bottle of poison in your chamber," Gloria said. "What've you been doing with the medicine for Edward?"

Simon surveyed his wife, unruffled by her accusations. "So hysterical, my treasure," he murmured in a parody of tenderness. "You're not well, Gloria. Perhaps you need rest."

"Answer my question!" Gloria trembled as she approached the bale of hay. "Did you ever love Edward, even for a moment? Why did you have poison in your room?"

Simon smiled, a strange gleam in his eyes. "How could I love him?" he said coldly. "When I went to the slave quarters one day, a wise woman intercepted me. She looked at me with such pity. 'You are not a man,' she told me. 'Something is missing from your heart.' She said that she had seen a vision in her mirror. A son would be born to me one day. She said that son would grow to be stronger than me. 'A weakling child will be worth more than you'll ever be. He will grow amid the slaves and the free, and he will bring liberation to those in captivity.' "

Thick silence descended. Even the crickets stilled their concert. Simon stared at Gloria's stricken face and smiled contemptuously. "You gullible fool. You never suspected a thing. It was so simple to deceive you. The poison was easy to acquire. Enough money, and you can procure anything and buy anyone's silence. Necessity breeds ingenuity, you see. I only give him small amounts. The demand for medicine continues even as he weakens. The more medicine that is needed, the more jewels I acquire."

Simon rose to his feet. "Why did you meddle in my affairs? You'll regret—" He gasped as a severe spasm of drowsiness hit him.

"Are you sleepy? You'll grow even sleepier." Gloria bowed her head with sorrow. "I loved you, Simon. I wanted to help you find the jewels so that we could finally make

Edward well. I could give you no more children. I wanted—
"

"Exactly!" Simon snarled. "You're worth nothing. I never believed that witch's prediction until Edward was born. A sickly, mewling brat! I looked into his whey-colored face and saw a reflection of myself." His face contorted with rage. "I won't be a weakling, do you hear me? I—" Another spasm of drowsiness seized him, and Simon fell to his knees. "What did you give me?" he whispered, his words slurred.

Gloria smiled. "You did it to yourself," she said. "Apple butter's always been your favorite. I only regret it's merely a sleeping draught and nothing stronger."

She watched as Simon collapsed on the ground. She turned to the stable door. *He'll awaken at dawn*, she said to herself. She had to be on her way as soon as possible. Isaac's words filled her mind. Hart Spring lay to the north across a river. Look for the hand in the sky, the hand that holds a drinking cup.

There was one more thing to do before she left.

CHAPTER THIRTEEN

"We get to help Mama gather flowers today," Annika said, splashing the dishwater around in her excitement.

Bianca nodded as she cleared away the breakfast dishes, but she was distracted. "Maybe we'll find some roses," she said.

Annika grinned. "And daisies. I love to make daisy chains."

Bianca did not answer. Unease wrapped itself around her shoulders. She grew more homesick every day. Even though Hart Spring felt more like home than anywhere, she missed Priscilla and Mabel terribly. She also could not rid herself of the feeling that there was something she had left undone. She knew this feeling grew from her worry for Edward.

A knock sounded on the cabin door. Annika turned to Bianca with a puzzled frown. "No one knocks here," she said. "Everyone knows everyone." She turned toward the door.

"Wait," Bianca said quickly. "Let's fetch George and Louise first."

Annika nodded and went to the adjoining room.

From outside, a reedy child's voice said, "I'm hungry." The voice was stronger than Bianca remembered it ever being, but she knew it immediately. Her heart pounding, she hurried to the door and opened it.

Four people stood outside. Bianca cried out with joy and flung herself into Priscilla's arms.

Priscilla grasped Bianca tightly. She was trembling. "My darling! My sweet dove!" She finally held Bianca at arm's length and stared into her eyes. "Thank the Creator you were led here," she breathed.

Bianca blinked rapidly. "George and Louise told me their story," she said. "You're George's sister. I missed you so much!" She turned to Mabel and Isaac.

Isaac gave Bianca a tentative smile. "I'm sorry, child," he said. "I had to do what I could to keep you safe."

Bianca shifted her attention to the little boy fidgeting impatiently beside them. "Edward," she said softly. "It's so wonderful to see you walking. You're looking so well." His cheeks were flushed with life, and he gazed around him with interest.

"I'm hungry," Edward repeated.

"What's this?" George's voice boomed. Bianca turned to him with a smile. George stared at the assembled people. His face crumpled, and he fell into Priscilla's arms. Sister and brother embraced, both of them shaking with sobs. After a long moment, George stepped back and cleared his throat.

George surveyed Edward, his brow furrowing with concern. "Seems a storytime is in order," he said gruffly.

"Not until after the child eats." Louise appeared behind her husband. "No one who comes to my house will stay hungry long. Annika, go fetch some bread and cheese."

Annika nodded, her face crumpling as she turned to obey her mother. She blinked a few times.

"I'll come with you," Bianca said quickly. She followed Annika to the small annex that served as a pantry. "What's wrong?" she asked gently.

Annika shook her head with a sigh. "You'll go away now," she said sadly.

Bianca frowned. "Not just yet," she said. "And even if I went away, I'd never forget you."

"But they've come here now," Annika said. "They have a free boy with them. Someone will look for him. They could get in trouble. Would you leave then? I'll miss you."

Bianca hugged Annika tightly. She looked around the small room. "I wish I could stay here," she said. "If there were only a way to be in two places at once!"

"I feel like I did the day I had to let Prickles go," Annika sniffled.

This was too much! Bianca burst out laughing. "You're saying I remind you of a hedgehog?"

Finally, Annika laughed and managed a small grin.

"Girls, the bread is already baked," Louise called. "Are you making a fresh loaf?"

The girls retrieved the supplies. "I know you have to go. I have to let you go if you want to," Annika said. "I'm glad the cheese lady came to the market last week. You get to have some more before you leave."

Bianca tousled Annika's hair. "You'll be all right," she said. "I promise. You're in Hart Spring, and you're—" Her voice stopped as realization pummeled her. Imbecile! She was an imbecile! Why hadn't she thought of this before?

"Priscilla!" Bianca ran into the adjoining room, causing the pewter dishes to rattle on their shelves. "You're safe here. You're free!"

Priscilla looked up with a wan smile. "Yes," she said, but her voice shook. "We are free according to the law of land boundaries, but I'm afraid—"

As if on cue, the cabin door opened. A burly man stepped across the threshold. George rose to face the man.

"Governor Charles," he said. "What brings you here so early in the day?"

"George, there's trouble in the marketplace," Charles said, his face lined with worry. "An intruder claims a free child was kidnapped by some runaways." He scanned the room, his eyes alighting on Edward. The boy's pale skin gleamed. The man surveyed the newcomers assembled around the table. "You all must come with me," he said brusquely.

Priscilla and Isaac exchanged frightened looks. "We have an explanation. The child was in danger," Isaac said.

Governor Charles inclined his head. "You'll have a chance to defend yourselves," he said. "Come along."

CHAPTER FOURTEEN

The makeshift market stood near the river. Vendors' tables were pushed back, and a platform was erected.

As Bianca entered the market, her heart skipped a beat. Father was seated in a chair flanked by two burly guards. His expression was livid.

Governor Charles gestured to the platform. "The accused must stand and face the accuser," he said. "Everyone else may be part of the audience."

Bianca watched helplessly as Priscilla, Isaac, and Mabel stepped onto the platform. Why had Edward come with them to Hart Spring? Something was wrong.

Priscilla and Isaac boldly approached Simon. They did not avert their gazes from his murderous stare. Only Mabel hung back. Bianca was startled to see that Mabel was shaking.

"Strangers," Charles intoned, "you have come to our land in search of refuge. Yet you bring a free child with you. This man claims that you drugged him and took his son away. If you have engaged in such an unlawful act, the sentence is immediate expulsion from this community. What have you to say in your defense?"

Isaac turned to Charles. "What he says is true," he said. "But the child was slowly being poisoned. This man cares nothing for his son. We have proof." He gestured to Priscilla.

She withdrew a strange object from her garment. A beautiful decoration of applewood shimmered in her hand. A princess struggled in the coils of a dragon. Priscilla removed the comb from the princess' hair. Bianca gazed at the remnants of crimson powder that were revealed.

"I retrieved this from the child's nursery," Priscilla said.

Charles frowned. "What is this strange object?" he inquired.

Isaac gestured to Mabel. Shaking, the girl stepped forward. "It's a mobile that hung from the ceiling. It holds a container that can be used for making a room smell pleasant. This container held poison," she said, her voice barely audible.

"She's lying." Bianca heard Father's familiar, deep-toned voice. It held a note of amusement. "My wife adores cosmetics and perfumes. It's a gift for her that I had especially made by a peddler." He sneered at Priscilla. "The ugly wretch must have stolen it in addition to my son."

Bianca gasped as if she'd been slapped. She watched as Priscilla raised a shaking hand to cover her face. Isaac took Priscilla's hand and glared at Simon. A rumble of angry voices filled the air.

Charles turned to Simon with a frown. "You will have an opportunity to tell your side of the story," he said harshly. "And you will refrain from name-calling. Everyone is given dignity here."

Bianca noticed that Mabel's head rose a little higher. Her voice grew stronger. "He shut me in the boy's nursery and used this evil instrument to put me to sleep. It was a trap for Mother. He wanted her to tell him where my sister was."

"Your sister?"

Mabel nodded. "She is free," she said firmly. "She had nothing to do with this."

But it wasn't true. If Mabel had been poisoned, it had everything to do with her. Mabel had called her sister, and Bianca knew that Mabel spoke the truth. Hadn't she herself felt drawn to Mabel all her life? They were indeed sisters, bound together forever. The yarn was not a binding of blood but a yarn of superior strength, the yarn of love. That skein also bound her to Priscilla.

Bianca trembled violently as she stepped forward. She saw Mabel desperately shaking her head, but she ignored her. "Here I am, Father," she said. The people murmured among themselves.

Clearing her throat, she turned and addressed the assembled crowd. "May I relate a tale?"

"Please do," the people chorused.

"Will you listen well?"

"Weave for us your word spell."

"Creator, give my words grace. Let my tale enliven this place." She clapped three times.

The people clapped four times. "Spin, spin, spin. Weave a tale of glory," they chorused.

Bianca stared at Father's face. He glared at her. Once again, she turned to the crowd. They were smiling encouragingly. She saw Priscilla's smile and Mabel's and Isaac's. Then she saw Annika. The girl raised her hand in a gesture of encouragement. Perhaps love's skein stretched even farther than she thought. Perhaps she belonged somewhere after all. Tears of gratitude coursed down Bianca's cheeks as she spoke.

"Once there was a girl who loved her father very much. He took her on picnics and gave her her favorite treat, apple butter. He called her his sweet princess. But the father always had a task for the girl to do. She had to listen to the music of the earth and tell him where its treasure lay buried. 'You must help my son,' the father said. 'I will buy a medicine that will cure his sickness. I will sell the jewels you hear and obtain enough money to have the medicine made.' The girl listened eagerly and told her father where to find the jewels.

"But the girl had to listen more and more. She grew weak, and the earth was losing life. Its energy drained away as the father took and took. The girl's energy left her. Her brother was always ill, and the father said the girl must try harder. But she could never satisfy him.

"Then one day, the girl was sent away from the land. She found freedom and strength in a place of peace. While in this place, the girl learned a horrible truth: she had not been helping her brother. She had been tricked. Her father had only wanted the jewels for himself. She learned that many people had died to satisfy her father's greed.

"The girl's mother and sister found her in her new home. The land welcomed them, along with the girl's brother and the one who had brought him."

Bianca gazed over the crowd.

Finally, the people spoke as one: "Thank you for the tale you have spun."

Bianca wiped away her tears. "Thank you for listening."

CHAPTER FIFTEEN

T his girl has exposed her heart for us that we all might understand what she has lost and what she has gained," Charles informed the crowd. "She has found refuge here, as have these others." He gazed at Simon with fury in his eyes. "If there is proof of the girl's story, we will punish you with the harshest sentence that is in our power to inflict. Have you anything to say in your defense?"

Simon smiled, his eyes blazing with amused fire. "There is nothing to say except that they are all liars. When they are released to me, I will make them suffer."

Bianca trembled more than ever, but she approached the platform and stepped upon it. She stood beside Priscilla, Isaac, and Mabel. She turned to Father. He looked upon her with hatred.

"If they must suffer, then I shall suffer too," she said hoarsely. Nausea clawed at her stomach. "I'll listen to the earth everyday if need be. Please spare everyone else. Please let them remain here."

"Wait." Governor Charles gestured for Priscilla to step forward. "Hand me the trinket you hold," he instructed. Priscilla did so. Charles inclined the container toward Simon. "If this concoction is merely perfume as you say, you will have no objection to smelling it."

Simon blinked, drawing back from the man's penetrating stare. "I see no purpose in continuing this sham of an interrogation," he said. "Release the slaves to me and relinquish my son. We will leave this place and cause you no further trouble."

Charles smiled. "It's a simple request," he said reflectively. "The only possible reason for your refusal is that the concoction is not what you claim."

Murmurs filled the crowd, and feet shuffled on the path. "He may not want to smell it, but I shall," a voice said.

Bianca gasped as Stepmother made her way through the crowd. She was dressed in black, as if she were in mourning, and no cosmetics adorned her face. Lines of despair were etched onto her skin. She was holding a box in her hand.

Gloria approached the platform and pointed a shaking finger at Simon. "I am his wife," she said, "and the boy is my son. I ask that you allow Edward to stay here where it is safe. I have brought something to pay you for the trouble." She held out the box and opened the lid.

Blinding light filled the marketplace, and Bianca gasped. An abundant array of jewels gleamed before her: sparkling Hart's Tears that shone with dazzling light. *Here!* The jewels whispered in her mind. *We are here.*

Simon tried to rise from the chair, but the guards restrained him.

"What is the meaning of this?" Charles asked.

"There are numerous boxes of this sort in my husband's bedchamber. I have seen them with my own eyes," Gloria said, her voice choked with tears. "I believed he was using the jewels the slaves procured to buy medicine for our son, but he was not." She turned to Priscilla and pointed to the mobile. "Give me the container," she instructed.

Priscilla shook her head. "No, Mistress."

Gloria frowned. "Obey me at once," she said. "I am a fool deserving of death. I have failed Edward and everyone else. These people want proof. They shall have it."

"That is not necessary," Charles said calmly. "I have seen enough." He turned to the crowd. "What say all of you? Is the accuser deserving of punishment?"

The crowd turned to the platform. "Let him be buried within a dragon's den," someone called. The crowd shouted in approval.

Charles nodded and raised a hand in a gesture of finality. "Hart Spring was purchased by the blood of many," he said solemnly. "The story we all know of the hart who stood between the escaping slaves and their pursuers to protect them is a story that immortalizes the many slaves who let themselves be killed so that others might live."

He pointed to Simon. "Therefore, as slaves have died while obtaining the wealth you seek, you will be bound and placed in one of the mines. Perhaps it will stand for some time, or perhaps it will not. Either way, you will be surrounded by the treasure you seem to love so." He bowed his head pityingly. "We will give you an opportunity to repent of your actions. Leave this land and swear never to return, and all will be forgotten."

Simon rose to his feet. The guards made no effort to stop him. "You think you can keep me away? No one will believe your word over mine. I'll summon the proper authorities, and you will suffer beyond imagining," he hissed. He lunged at Gloria. Bianca reached out, clamping her hand onto Simon's wrist.

Simon turned to her. "You dare to touch me, filthy traitor? I regret you were ever born!" He bestowed upon Bianca a stare that sent fear coursing through her body. "You will indeed listen for me, and I will take what I want.

You cannot tell me what I can and cannot do. These others will come back with us."

Simon wrenched himself from Bianca's grasp. He feverishly groped for Gloria's arm. "Interfering witch! You have no right to touch my things! Those are my sister's tears! She left me, and all I have is the reminder of her weakness. Without that reminder, how can I be strong? How can I make my father proud? Restore to me my property!" Bianca realized that Father was trying to take the box of jewels.

Isaac raised a meaty hand, intercepting Simon's own. "Say your daughter's name," Isaac growled, his voice sounding like the quaking earth.

Simon sneered. "You dare to order me to do something? I am master, and you are nothing! She has no name."

"Say it!" Isaac grabbed Simon's wrist and twisted it, causing Simon to bellow in pain.

"I-I will not say it! She is weak, and she is nothing to me!" Simon finally stammered, his cheeks growing ashen with fear.

Isaac turned to Priscilla who was standing beside him. "Then I claim Bianca as my daughter," he said. He released Simon's arm in disgust, and the man fell to his knees, all bravado gone.

"I claim her as my sister," Annika called from the crowd. "We all claim her."

Bianca looked upon the crowd. Everyone smiled at her and raised their hands in a gesture of welcome.

"We claim the sojourners who brought the young boy here," Charles said. "And we claim the child and his mother if they desire to stay." His voice boomed with authority. He nodded to the family on the platform. "You may all step down now."

His steely gaze turned to Simon, who still cowered on the ground. "As for you, dragon, I think your lies will not withstand the truth when the proper evidence is presented." He surveyed the vast crowd, his eyes resting longest on Gloria. She nodded at him. Then he held the mobile aloft. He addressed Simon once more. "Since you refuse mercy, prepare to suffer judgment."

Guards materialized from every direction. Simon was bound in chains. He cursed and struggled, but to no avail.

Bianca stared over the crowd, not believing her eyes. Her family surged around her, and she suddenly knew that she was home.

One woman stood apart, her ravaged face weary but her head held high. Hesitantly, Bianca gestured for Gloria to join them. After a moment, Gloria did so.

Trembling, she handed the box of jewels to Bianca. "You were right to call me ugly," she whispered. "I sought to have you killed so that I might obtain your gift of listening to the earth's music. I was foolish and desperate. I cannot repair what I have done."

Bianca stared at Gloria for a long moment. Then she looked toward her new family. She shook her head. "I was wrong," she said. "You are more beautiful than I thought." She handed the box back to Gloria. "Won't you please use this to help other slaves find their way here? I learned of a store where a man and his wife help slaves find freedom. The wife's name is Janet. Perhaps she can help you."

Gloria hesitated for a moment then closed her hand over the box. She nodded. "I will go back across the river," she said, "and I will do what I can to mend the evil that's been done. They have claimed Edward, so he will remain here until I return."

Stepmother and stepdaughter embraced.

Epilogue

*D*o you think that Priscilla will want spice cake for her wedding?" Annika grinned at Bianca as the girls gathered flowers for a breakfast centerpiece. The perfume of the roses tickled the girls' noses and caused them to sneeze.

Bianca laughed. "Spice cake is Mother's favorite, so I hope so." She thought with rapture of Mother's wedding preparations. Priscilla and Isaac would be wed at the end of the month.

The earth had not called to Bianca since the night after Simon's sentencing. On that night, she had dreamed of the earth. It had rumbled and quaked. Then a panicked scream had filled her ears. Bianca knew without having to be told that the mine where Simon had been imprisoned had collapsed.

Bianca hoped she would hear the earth again in time. If she did, she would tell someone who would take only what was necessary. Perhaps she could use the jewels to bring other slaves here. There were endless possibilities.

Gloria had been true to her word. Slaves from Simon's plantation and from other areas were coming to Hart Spring in droves. The jewels Simon had stolen were being put to good use. Edward had had no further bouts of sickness.

Bianca smiled at Annika. "Let's ask George if we can go fishing today," she said. "Edward loves catfish."

Annika grinned. "I'll bet Papa and Isaac will be glad to have a rest from building on the extra rooms to the cabin."

Bianca nodded. "I'm sure they will. Come on." She took Annika's hand, and the girls skipped toward the cabin. Now that eight people resided there, the family was working to add extra room.

The girls waved as they passed Edward. The little boy was carrying an empty water pail. "Morning, Edward," Bianca called.

Edward waved back and grinned. "Louise says I'm strong enough to fetch the water myself today," he said proudly.

Even at so young an age, the boy carried himself with regal grace. Bianca knew he would grow up to become a great man. She watched Edward skip toward the river. She bowed her head with sadness as she thought of the father she had lost. Then she smiled as she breathed a prayer of thanksgiving for the family she had found.

As she approached the cabin, Bianca sang softly. Her voice was a pale shadow of Mother's, but her joy made the song sound more beautiful than any dove's refrain:

> *Across the dividing river,*
> *Amid wildflowers' golden gleam,*
> *Lies a land bought by brutal means,*
> *A land where we have come.*

ACKNOWLEDGEMENTS

I am indebted to authors Julius Lester and Tim Tingle, whose books entitled *Day of Tears* and *Crossing Bok Chitto: A Choctaw Tale of Freedom and Friendship* sparked the inspiration for this story. Hart Spring is different from anything I've ever written, and I was truly amazed at how vividly the characters appeared in my mind. It is incredible how authors' works might light candles of inspiration for other ideas.

"Snow White" is my favorite of the Grimm Brothers' stories despite its many disturbing themes. It is, in my opinion, one of the most complex of the Grimms' collected stories. I relate to Snow White because, like her, I was sent away from home at a very early age and had to adjust to new surroundings and people. To me, "Snow White" is not a romance but a tale of finding where you belong even if innocence is lost. So, I wanted to focus on family in my retelling as opposed to creating a romantic tale. I am eternally grateful to my own family, who have made sacrifices too numerous to mention in order that I might learn to walk the path Jesus has established for my life. God bless you all.

I would like to thank Hannah Williams, who took the time to design an incredible cover for this story collection. She is talented, and she is very accommodating. And I am grateful to Savannah Jezowski, who did amazing work on interior layout design. I am grateful to Stephanie Ricker, an amazing editor whose insights helped me to polish these tales and make them shine. I am thankful for the fairy tale writing contests of Rooglewood Press, for without them, these stories would not have been written.

Finally, I would like to say that I was nervous writing *Hart Spring,* as I did not feel qualified to write about the theme of slavery. However, the idea was so strong in my mind that I had to write it down. I researched slave settlements and abolitionists but know there is always more research to be done. The fight for freedom was not as simple as this tale might imply. I tried to create a fantasy world that had some roots in American history but was totally its own place. I do not mean this story to be historical fiction, but a fairy tale reflective of the truth. Any errors in this story are entirely my own.

ABOUT THE AUTHOR

Meredith Leigh Burton is a voracious devourer of fairy tales. She is a motivational speaker, writer, and teacher. She attended the Tennessee School for the Blind and Middle Tennessee State University. She received a degree in English and theater. Meredith hopes to convey through her stories that those with differences can contribute much to the world. She resides in Lynchburg, Tennessee.